# BLOOM

*NEW YORK TIMES* BESTSELLING AUTHOR

## DEBORAH BLADON

# *Also by Deborah Bladon*

# Chapter 1

## *Athena*

My shop, Wild Lilac, seems to be the place all the hot guys in Manhattan come to when they're looking to impress their certain someone with flowers.

Today is a perfect example of that. One of my first customers this morning was a hotshot hockey player. I only know that because I saw his face on a billboard in Times Square during the playoffs last season.

After he bought and paid for the perfect bouquet for his special lady, a looker in a suit strolled through the door.

It took him over an hour to choose the arrangement he wanted. I was happy to oblige since it cost a small fortune. The flowers will be delivered tomorrow before he goes to the yoga studio his girlfriend owns to drop to one knee to ask her to spend her life with him.

I look over at the man who walked in less than a minute ago.

He's sexy-as-sin.

His dark blond hair is pushed back from his face and skimming the collar of his black button-down shirt. The sleeves are rolled up to his elbows, so the black and gray tattoos that cover his muscular forearms are visible.

He's giving off a semi-corporate vibe since he's dressed in black pants and shoes.

I turn to the side to stop myself from staring at him.

"Excuse me?"

If there ever was a perfect voice for phone sex, it belongs to this man.

I look over at his face. His jaw is covered with a trimmed beard. His blue eyes pierce through me as he stares at me.

The man is a gorgeous giant. He must be at least six-foot-five.

"Can I help you?" I ask cheerfully from behind my checkout counter because swooning over the clientele will not pay the rent on this place.

"I need some flowers." He huffs out a laugh. "Nice flowers. I want something extra special for the woman I'm seeing."

Something deflates inside of me. It's not as though I was expecting him to be in my floral boutique to buy a bouquet for his mom. That mad rush happens in May. It's late September. The bulk of my recent orders have been gestures of undying devotion, new baby arrivals, birthdays, or sadly, red rose heavy arrangements to honor the recently departed.

"Are you celebrating something?" I ask not only because that will help me determine what type of bouquet to suggest, but curiosity is a motivating factor too.

"I'm celebrating her."  His tone softens. "She's an incredible woman."

*She's a lucky woman.*

His eyes skim the front of the black sweater I'm wearing. "What's your name?"

That's not a question I'm asked often since I usually have a nametag pinned to my chest, but this sweater and sharp objects don't play well together.

"Athena."

"Nice." He flashes me a smile. "I'm Wolf."

"Wolf?" I question back because that has to be a nickname. "Your name is Wolf?"

His hand jumps to his chin. Smoothing his fingertips over his beard, he huffs out a laugh. "It is. I'm Liam Wolf."

"Liam," I repeat his first name because it suits him perfectly in some abstract, unexplainable way.

The breadth of his shoulders and his height make him intimidating to look at, but his eyes and the warmth in his voice tell a different story.

I'm running a business, so I go to the heart of the matter. "What kind of flowers are you thinking of?"

"Whatever takes your breath away," he says.

Never mind the flowers; that statement did the trick.

Speechless, I stare at him.

He bows his chin. "I'm looking for an arrangement that will surprise the hell out of my girlfriend. It has to be unique. Do you think you can handle that, Athena?"

I can handle anything, even creating beautiful bouquets for men like him to give to other women.

"I'm up for the job." I smile.

Sliding a credit card and a sealed envelope toward me, he takes a pause. "Her name and address are written on there. I need that and the flowers sent to her today."

All of my deliveries have already gone out, and it's nearing five o'clock.

"My delivery cut-off is at two." I glance down at the large silver watch on his wrist. "I can have this in her hands tomorrow."

"It has to be today." He leans both of his palms on the counter. "I'll pay extra if you can get it to her before eight."

Who am I to stand in the way of true love? I have nothing planned for tonight, so I do my good deed for the day. "I can take it to her personally. No extra charge."

His eyes scan my face. "If you can make that happen, I'll be forever in your debt."

I set to work writing out an invoice for an elaborate arrangement of the most expensive flowers I have in stock. If I'm going to do this tonight, I might as well do it right. I hope the woman on the receiving end of the bouquet and the note realizes just how lucky she is.

"You'll confirm once they're in Wren's hand?"

I glance at the front of the envelope and the masculine handwriting.

Even the way he writes his girlfriend's name is sexy.

WREN HOLSON.

Beneath it is an address in Tribeca.

My gaze shifts to his handsome face. "The recipient usually confirms the delivery in a phone call or text to the sender."

That goes without saying. Most people who receive flowers can't wait to thank the person who sent them. I overheard my fair share of those calls when I worked at a floral shop during summer break in high school. I handled any deliveries that could be made on foot. It saved the shop owner a nice chunk of change, and it gave me insight into how much an unexpected gift of fragrant blossoms can instantly alter a person's mood.

"Wren has a shoot that starts at seven." He taps his finger on the envelope. "She's a photographer. This is her studio address. It might take her a minute to get in touch with me after you deliver the flowers, so I'd appreciate confirmation. A text will do just fine since I'll be busy with a couple of appointments at my office tonight."

I push a pad of paper and a pen at him. "Jot down your number on here."

His lips curve into a smile. "Sure thing, Athena."

Out of the corner of my eye, I watch as he writes out the digits. I'll program it into my phone for the night, but by tomorrow morning it will be history.

I finish up the invoice and slide it toward him. "Have a look over this and see if that works for you."

His gaze catches mine. Without a glance down, he studies my face. "Charge it to my card and add a twenty percent tip."

I already added a generous rush fee to the total, but since he hasn't looked at the invoice, he doesn't realize that.

I play to the moment as I pick up his card to run it through the register. "I'll add ten percent to this order. You can tip me twenty on the next bouquet."

"The next?" His brows perk.

"Once you see how grateful your girlfriend is, you'll be back."

I must have said that line hundreds of times since I opened the shop last year, but today it feels different. There's more hope in my words than confidence. I'd like to see him again, even if it's just for the innocent banter when he orders Wren Holson another bouquet.

"I have no doubt I'll be back." He flashes me a gorgeous smile. "I'll leave you to work your magic. Thanks for everything, Athena."

"Thank you, Liam."

"I don't hear that often," he says, lowering his voice.

An ache settles somewhere deep inside of me from the rasp in his tone. "You don't hear what often?"

"My name." He pauses. "Most people call me Wolf."

I tilt my chin up, taking another long look at his handsome face. "I like the name Liam."

"Do you?" he asks with a cock of his brow. "I like your name too. What's your last name?"

I give it up because a glance at the store's website reveals that tidbit of information. "Millett. Athena Millett."

"That's beautiful." He leans forward. "I've never met anyone named Athena before."

I rub a hand over my forehead, suddenly aware of what I must look like to him. I've been at work since six a.m., and it shows. My long golden brown hair is cinched up in a tight ponytail, but a few wayward strands have fallen loose. The black liner I applied around my blue eyes has to be smudged by now, along with my mascara. My soft pink lipstick found a new home on the metal straw of my water bottle.

I drag myself back to the reason he's here. "I should get started on Wren's arrangement."

He steals a glance at his watch. "I need to get back to my office. Thanks again."

Shoving a hand through his hair, he turns and walks out of my store, leaving me with the task of creating something beautiful for his girlfriend.

Dropping my gaze to the counter in front of me, I realize he left me with something else.

His credit card.

It looks like I'll see Liam Wolf again very soon.

# Chapter 2

### *Athena*

Wren Holson stares at me with her big green eyes.

A toss of her dark brown hair over her shoulder only adds to her attitude at the moment.

My first mistake was barging into the middle of the mommy and son photo shoot that's going on.

I can blame that on her assistant. He was on his way out of her studio when I showed up. The enormous floral arrangement in my hands didn't faze him. He pointed at a pretty brunette wearing a teal jumpsuit and holding a camera.

I sauntered over with a big smile on my face and promptly sent the little boy nestled in his mother's arms into a crying fit.

The flowers scared the hell out of him.

They've been a pain since I left my shop and hopped onto the subway to come here.

I poked more people than I care to admit as I swung the bouquet from arm-to-arm, trying desperately not to injure anyone.

Wren's gaze drops to the envelope in her hands.

I got her to take that, but so far she hasn't reached for the flowers. I shove them at her for the third time. "I'm sorry again for the interruption, Ms. Holson. I hope you enjoy these."

She doesn't make a move to take them from me. "Did Wolf send you here?"

I sneak a peek at the blonde woman dressed in blue, holding her now-quiet son. "He did."

Sliding a pink manicured fingernail under the seal of the envelope, Wren sighs. "Give me a minute, will you?"

*For what?*

I've already overstayed my welcome. I should be out the door and texting Liam by now. I need to tell him that the delivery was a success and that I have his credit card in the front pocket of my jeans.

Wren's gaze flits over my face before it settles on the gold locket hanging around my neck. "Wait right here."

I stand in place as the heels of her sky-high black boots tap out an impatient rhythm on the hardwood floor with every step she takes away from me.

"Those flowers are all kinds of gorgeous." The woman bouncing the baby in her arms smiles at me. "Did her boyfriend send those to her?"

I don't think I'm divulging any secrets by nodding my head.

"What florist do you deliver for?" She asks with a tilt of her chin. "My mom's birthday is creeping up. It's her big six-o, so I want to surprise her with something like that."

I glance at the door that Wren disappeared behind at the back of the studio. Since I have the time, I might as well make the most of it.

Balancing the bouquet in my left arm, I fish in my tote for one of my business cards. I don't hand out a lot of them, but my brother insisted I order a box when I set up shop. He's not only my silent partner but my mentor too.

I yank a small white card out of one of the compartments inside of my bag. "I own Wild Lilac."

Taking a few steps forward, I drop my card in her outstretched hand.

She scans the violet-colored text. "I think I just found my new favorite florist."

*I'll never get tired of hearing those words.*

"Hey." The sound of Wren's voice turns my attention to the back of the studio.

I raise a hand and smile as if we're old friends. "Can I put these on that table over there?"

Wren's gaze shifts to the rectangular table covered with camera equipment, notepads, and a computer. "No. You're taking those with you."

Darting to her feet, the woman who is holding the baby asks the obvious question before I have a chance to. "Why is she taking those flowers with her?"

Wren stabs a corner of the envelope I gave her into the top of my hand.

I look down. Her name has a line of red ink slashed through it. Written under that in the same crimson shade is one word.

*Wolf.*

"Give this to him," she says when I take the envelope. "Give him the flowers too."

I flip the envelope over in my hand. The only thing holding the seal in place is a small piece of blue tape in the center of it.

10

"I wrote on the back of his note," she explains, her voice even. "I don't want flowers. He shouldn't have sent them."

"Maybe you should call him?" I suggest quietly.

That perks both her brows. "I said everything I want to say in my note. It's over. I'm done. I should have ended it weeks ago."

My gaze lands beyond her shoulder on the blonde woman. The expression on her face must mirror the one on mine. I'm shocked. This has never happened to me.

"You can go." Wren dismisses me with a flick of her wrist. "I'm busy. Sorry for your trouble."

I stuff the envelope in my tote and turn my back to her. Taking a deep breath, I march across the studio, wondering how in the hell I got stuck in the middle of this.

\*\*\*

Liam Wolf didn't answer my call or respond to any of the three text messages I sent to him since leaving Wren's studio. I could have waited until tomorrow to get in touch with him, but that comes with a risk.

The risk is that if he reaches out to Wren tonight, he won't have a full understanding of where his relationship stands.

It's not my job to give the envelope to him before the clock strikes midnight, but he seems like a decent guy. He deserves to know that Wren wrote him a note when she refused the flowers.

Running my fingers over the screen of my phone, I find what I'm looking for with a quick online search.

Liam's a grief counselor.

He works in a building on West 54th Street.

I plug in the numbers for his office phone.

By the third ring I expect it to go to voicemail, but a female voice answers. "Dehaven Center. Good evening. How may I help you?"

Stepping back from the street, I settle in a spot under the awning of a closed deli. It's not as though I'd need to shout over the noise of the traffic whizzing past, but this conversation feels like it deserves a modicum of respect.

"I need to speak to Liam Wolf."

I hope that I can convince him to meet me back at Wild Lilac so I can give him the envelope and his credit card. The flowers technically belong to him, so the choice of what to do with them is in his hands.

"Mr. Wolf is unavailable. May I take a message?"

"I have something that belongs to him," I explain to the woman on the other end of the call. "It's imperative that I give it to him tonight."

"Do you know where our office is located?" she chirps back in a happy tone.

Even though she can't see me, I nod. "I do."

"If you'd like, you can swing by and drop off whatever it is," she pauses. "I'll be sure it gets to him before he leaves for the day."

This is an answer to my prayer.

I won't have to be the bearer of bad news. I can dump everything in the lap of the woman I'm talking to.

"I'll be there in fifteen minutes," I say before ending the call.

This delivery debacle is almost over. After a quick stop at Liam's office, I'll be home free.

# Chapter 3

### *Athena*

"Oh, no." Audrey, the woman sitting behind the reception desk at Dehaven Center, shakes her head. "Are you saying that you tried to give these to his girlfriend, and she refused them?"

I nod. I explained the situation to her twice. The first time I could tell she wasn't paying attention. Her focus was on the screen of the phone in her hands.

When I plopped the enormous bouquet on her desk, she took notice, so I repeated my story word-for-word a second time.

"I thought Wren was the woman of his dreams," she mutters under her breath. "Why would she do this?"

I shrug as if the question was directed at me even though I know she's lost in thought.

I shove a hand into the front pocket of my jeans and tug out Liam's credit card. "He forgot this at my shop. Can you see to it that he gets this too?"

Her gaze floats over the card before it lands back on the envelope. "You said that she wrote him a note?"

I watch as she flips the envelope over. Her fingernail skims over the small piece of blue tape.

I lean forward. "Her note is in there. It's for his eyes only."

It's not my place to say that, but I swear that this woman is about ready to pull back the tape and read the message.

"Of course." She pushes the envelope to the side. "Did she say anything about what she was feeling?"

The compassion in her tone is unmistakable. Blonde curls bounce around her heart-shaped face. She's dressed in a cream suit with a pink blouse underneath. Her entire look gives off an air of calmness and serenity.

It makes sense since she's the first person to greet anyone who walks through the double glass doors of the Dehaven Center.

The reception area that I'm standing in is decorated in muted tones. There's soft music playing and the gray chairs that line the wall face a coffee table that is covered in magazines and pamphlets.

To the left is a corridor that's home to a series of doors. All of them are open except one.

I'm not about to offer her a replay of Wren's words, so I go with the easy answer. "She asked me to give the note and the flowers to him."

Audrey trails a fingertip over one of the petals of a yellow daylily. "These are breathtaking. Mr. Wolf has great taste, doesn't he?"

I glance over my shoulder at the bank of elevators beyond the glass doors before I level my gaze back on her face. "I need to go."

"I introduced them," she says, shoving to her feet. "Wren did my engagement photos and I've booked her for the wedding too."

She wiggles her left hand in the air, showing off a diamond and emerald ring.

"This isn't my first marriage, but who says you can't have it all the second time around?"

I'm not one to judge. If circumstances were different, I'd pitch my case to do the flowers for her wedding, but I'm only here to deliver bad news.

As if she's read my mind, she sighs. "Which florist do you work for? I'm looking for just the right person to handle the flowers for my special day."

My hand dives back into my tote. I yank out another business card. I haven't given out two in one day before.

"I own Wild Lilac." I drop the card in front of her. "I'd be honored to work with you on creating the perfect floral designs for your wedding."

It's a line I rehearsed over and over before I opened the shop. I don't have the best track record at appearing casual when I'm jumping up and down with joy internally.

Audrey gazes at my card before she slides it into one of the pockets of her suit jacket. "I'll call you this week and we'll set something up."

I've scored two new potential clients tonight. It's a big win I didn't see coming when I set out to deliver the bouquet to Wren.

"I look forward to that." I tap my fingers on her desk, knowing that I'll call her in a week if see hasn't reached out. "Thank you for taking care of the situation with Liam."

"Athena? What are you doing here?"

The sound of Liam's voice lures Audrey's gaze to the left. Mine follows.

Liam is standing next to an older man. It's obvious by the tissue in the man's hand and the redness of his eyes that he's been crying.

I look down not wanting to infringe on the man's privacy.

"I'll see you next week?" The man's voice is gentle and soft. "Same time?"

"Absolutely," Liam answers. "If you need to talk before then, call anytime."

Audrey lowers herself back into her chair as the man passes us both on his way out of the office and toward the elevators.

I'd follow his lead, but I doubt he'd appreciate the company on the ride down to the lobby.

"What's all this?" Liam's hand hovers over the flowers and his credit card. "You said you'd take care of the delivery tonight, Athena."

"She tried," Audrey interjects before I can say anything.

Liam's gaze finds mine. His brows pinch together. "Was there a problem?"

I motion toward the envelope near Audrey's hand. "Wren wrote you a note and asked me to get it to you along with the flowers. You forgot your credit card at my shop, so I thought I'd stop by here and drop everything off."

"That was my idea," Audrey pipes up. "I told Athena to come by when she called asking to speak with you. I knew you'd want to deal with this tonight."

I have no problem letting her take credit for this hot mess.

After sliding the credit card into his pocket, Liam scoops up the envelope. Ripping it open, he flips the paper over twice before he scans what's written in red ink.

"What the hell?" he bites out under his breath.

Audrey cranes her neck to try and read anything that's in her view.

I drop my gaze because looking at the floor seems like the safest bet at the moment. That note is personal. I'm already too involved in this.

My timing may be off, but I need to get the hell out of here. I consider my next move. Do I offer my condolences? Is it better to leave without a word?

I don't know the protocol for walking out on a customer who just got dumped.

Audrey unwittingly jumps into the role of my savior. "I assume you'd like some time alone, so Athena and I will leave you be. You'll lock up?"

I toss her a look of gratefulness, but her gaze is pinned on Liam's face.

"Yes," he says curtly. "I'll see you tomorrow, Audrey."

I'm not offered anything but a quick glance from him.

I'll take it.

Anything is better than having to answer questions about Wren's demeanor or what she said before she sent me packing.

Audrey shoulders a dark blue purse and rounds her desk headed toward the double glass doors that lead to the bank of elevators. Silently following her, I steal one last look at Liam.

Our eyes lock for the briefest of moments before he turns and starts back down the corridor, leaving the note and the flowers behind.

# Chapter 4

### *Athena*

An unexpected loud rap on the locked door of my floral shop sends the glass vase in my hand crashing to the ground.

"Dammit," I whisper under my breath even though I'm the only one here.

I'm alone inside the store every morning until I unlock the doors at nine a.m. sharp. That's when Leanna Pearsall arrives with two piping hot teas in her hands.

She's a wizard when it comes to floral arranging.

Years of her life have been spent inside this shop. Leanna worked for the previous owner. Part of the sale agreement was that I'd employ Leanna for six hours a day, five days a week. Her husband, Al, handles all of the store's deliveries when he pops by to pick up Leanna after her shift.

The rest of his day is spent being an Uber driver.

They balance their time so at least one of them is home when their three kids aren't in school.

A quick glance at the clock on the wall keeps me in place.

There's a sign posted on the door that clearly states when Wild Lilac is open for business. I use the precious early morning hours to work on orders and accept a daily delivery from my floral supplier.

That's already happened, so the person still banging their hand against the door has to be an overly eager customer.

Just as I reach down to grab one of the large shards of glass, the phone sitting on the checkout counter starts ringing.

It jars me enough that I turn toward the sound quickly, too quickly.

A jagged corner of the piece of glass in my hand tears across my finger.

A single drop of blood falls on the white tile by my feet.

Pressing my finger into the palm of my other hand, I head for the checkout counter and the box of tissues that are always there.

Leanna was the one who suggested we have tissues available to customers. Ordering flowers can be an emotional experience for some people, especially those who are looking for a bouquet to send to a person who lost a loved one.

By the time I open my hand to grab a tissue, blood has pooled in my palm.

I outgrew my fear of blood somewhere around the time one of my younger brothers cracked his chin against the sidewalk in front of our townhouse.

I stepped up to the plate, dragging him back inside even though he was already five inches taller than me.

I cleaned the wound, bandaged it up, and took him to the hospital in a taxi.

He needed four stitches.

I deserved a medal for overcoming my fear of blood.

My seventeen-year-old self was proud that I'd played the part of a responsible adult.

Today, six years later, I'm still trying to master that role.

*Some days are easier than others.*

I glance down at a drop of blood that has soaked into the thigh of my dark wash jeans.

I can trade them out for the extra pair of jeans I have stored in my locker in the back room.

My wardrobe planning is interrupted by the persistent blare of a car alarm. I look toward the door of my shop. Whoever was knocking is gone, but I catch a glimpse of someone darting past on the sidewalk.

Dawn hasn't settled over Manhattan yet, but there are always people milling about. I start my daily walk here just after six. My first stop is to share a brief conversation with a bodega owner who is always sweeping the sidewalk outside his shop. In the dead of winter, when snow blankets the city, he trades the broom for a shovel, but he never fails to have a smile on his face regardless of the weather.

My last stop is at a bakery a block from here.

It doesn't open until seven, so I stand in front of the shuttered windows and breathe in the scent of freshly baked bread.

For such a large, crowded city, those moments offer a small-town feel that I once knew and still sometimes wish for.

The phone on the counter starts ringing again.

"What?" I ask in exasperation. "Who has a floral emergency at six-thirty in the morning?"

Swiping up the blood with a tissue, I reach for the phone. "Good morning. Wild Lilac. This is Athena speaking."

"Hey." A toe-curling male voice greets me. "Do you have a minute to talk to me?"

I'll give him as many minutes as he wants. Whoever he is, he's got a voice that I could listen to all day.

"Sure," I say. "What can I help you with?"

The low rumble of a chuckle flows out of him. "You can start by unlocking the door."

I look back at the door and the man peering into the shop with a hand perched over his forehead and a phone tucked against his ear.

I didn't think I'd see Liam Wolf again, yet here he is in the flesh waiting for me to open the door and let him in.

# Chapter 5

## *Liam*

Athena's gaze glides over my gray T-shirt and the faded jeans I put on after I showered an hour ago.

On any other weekday morning, I'd be prepping for a full day at the office, but my first appointment isn't until eleven.

Locking the door behind me, she twists in a circle sending her long hair flowing down her back.

"We don't open until nine," she says. "Why are you here?"

I glance down at her hand and the crumpled tissue she's holding. Tilting my head to get a better look, I spot a red stain. "Are you bleeding?"

"It's nothing." Her right hand darts behind her back. "I cut myself on a piece of glass."

"Let me see." I curl a finger in the air. "It looks bad."

Shaking her head, she points at an antique rectangular table set up next to a row of coolers with glass doors that house buckets filled with flowers. "I dropped a vase. It's a hazard of the job."

I look over at the shards of glass littering the floor. "That's a hazard of the job?"

The pink sweater she's wearing slides down her left shoulder to reveal bare skin. She doesn't make a move to readjust it.

"Your hand," I say, pointing a finger at her. "Let me see."

Reluctantly, she swings her arm forward. When she opens her hand, she bunches the tissue in her other fist. "See? I told you. It's nothing."

Her hand is small. It's delicate. A thin gold band circles her thumb.

A single drop of blood seeps out of the cut on her index finger.

"How deep is that?" I ask, reaching for her.

Her breath catches when I take her hand in mine, cradling it gently. "It's not deep enough for stitches."

I lean down to get a closer look.

She's right. It's shallow. My eye wanders over her palm, stopping at a half-inch scar that taints the perfect skin.

I circle the area with my fingertips. "This one was deeper. What happened here?"

Dabbing the tissue on the fresh cut, she laughs. "That's a carrot's fault."

I hold back a smile. "A carrot?"

Her eyes lock on mine. Nodding, she sighs. "I had a pet rabbit when I was a kid. I grabbed a carrot and a knife to make dinner for it. The knife ended up in my hand."

I wince. "That must have hurt like hell."

She shrugs, sending the sweater another half-inch down her shoulder. "I don't remember."

"You don't remember?"

Her head bows, a smiling playing on her full lips. "I passed out."

I cock a brow.

"The sight of blood used to make me lightheaded," she goes on. "When the knife pierced my skin, I hit the floor."

I look her over from head-to-toe. "It looks like you've worked through that. You're steady on your feet."

"It's all smoke and mirrors. I'm going to grab a bandage and wrap this up."

I step aside when she brushes past me headed back toward her work area.

I follow behind her, easily keeping up with her hurried pace.

Popping open a plastic container on a bench near the table, she yanks out a bandage. She unwraps it and has it around her finger in an instant.

Tossing the tissue and the bandage wrapper in the trash, she finally turns her full attention back to me. "How can I help you, Liam?"

I wish to fuck I knew. I left my apartment this morning in search of fresh air and I ended up in this neighborhood. I never expected to find Athena at work this early. She got stuck in the middle of a shitty situation last night because of me and I want to make that right.

I didn't anticipate that Wren would pull the plug on our relationship. We had our issues, but we were working through them. I thought we were headed toward better times, not a breakup.

Waiting for me to answer, Athena rounds the table, being mindful not to step on any pieces of the broken vase.

I do the same. I follow her lead when she crouches to pick up the glass.

The heels on her black boots are less than an inch. By my estimate, she's no more than five foot two or three. I've got more than a foot in height and a hundred pounds on her, but down here, face-to-face, we're on a level playing field.

"You don't have to clean up my mess for me," she says.

Reaching for a large piece of glass, I huff out a laugh. "It's the least I can do after wasting hours of your life last night."

Her hand lands on my wrist, stilling my movements. "You didn't waste my time."

I lock eyes with her. I know kindness when I see it. "I put you in a bad position last night. I'm sorry about that."

"Not bad," she corrects me with a lift of her brow. "Awkward. It was awkward, but there was a bright side to it."

Curiosity draws my brows up too. "I don't see a bright side."

"For me." She taps a finger to her chest. "Not you."

"Ouch." I fight back a smile. "That hurt."

She drops the jagged piece of glass in her hand. "Oh no. I didn't mean that."

A pink flush floods her cheeks. Studying her face, I realize that she's not wearing much makeup. I'm far from an expert, but it looks like a coat of mascara and a dab of something shiny on her lips.

"What did you mean?" I question back.

"I connected with some potential new customers last night." She tugs on the sweater, sliding it back up her shoulder. "One at the photo studio and another at your office."

She must be talking about Audrey, but I don't know if the other person is Wren. I won't ask. I've never chased after a woman once a relationship is over.

Why waste my time on someone who wants me to go to hell?

Wren's words in her note were crystal clear. I don't exist to her anymore, so I'll move on. Simple.

Picking up a piece of glass, I toss it into the wastebasket. "I'm glad to hear that."

Biting the corner of her lip, she looks into my eyes. "I'm sorry about what happened to you last night."

I can tell the sentiment is genuine, so I take it that way. "Thank you."

We finish cleaning the glass in silence. Once she's swept up the area, she turns to face me. "I'm still a little confused about why you came all the way down here so early in the morning. If it was to apologize, that's not necessary."

I don't know where the words come from, but I let them roll off my tongue. "I need another bouquet."

Her eyes widen. "For Wren? The bouquet I left with you last night should still be fine. The flowers haven't died, have they? They were all fresh when I put the arrangement together."

"I gave that bouquet to my neighbor."

"Your neighbor?"

"She's ten." I lean my hip against the table. "Her face lit up like it was Christmas Day."

Her expression softens. "That was kind of you."

"Her parents have been good to me," I admit. "They feed me when I forget to feed myself."

This conversation is unexpected, but it's so damn easy. I haven't felt this comfortable with anyone in a hell of a long time.

"I'd like to stop by later today and pick up something with roses for my mom." I point at a bucket of yellow roses in the display cooler behind her. "Yellow roses and throw in a few other flowers."

Athena glances back over her shoulder. "Is it her birthday?"

"Not today." I tug my wallet out of my back pocket. "I just want to surprise her."

"It's a sunshine bouquet," she says matter-of-factly.

Crossing my arms, I take the bait. "A sunshine bouquet? What's that?"

"It's an arrangement meant to bring sunshine to someone's day."

"A sunshine bouquet it is." I slide my credit card out of my wallet. "Dial it back from what you put together last night. I pissed off a few people on the subway when I unintentionally stabbed them in the back with that thing."

"You said you wanted something extra special." She shoots me a smile.

I raise both hands in surrender. "I did. Today I want something beautiful that I can control on the subway."

"What time will you pick it up?"

"I'll text you later to let you know." Rubbing my jaw, I clear my throat. "Ignore the texts I sent you earlier."

She pauses, looking over at her phone. "You texted me this morning?"

"Twice," I admit. "When you didn't respond, I realized you were probably asleep, so I came down here to slip a note under the door."

"You did?"

I straighten in place. "I feel guilty that you had to play messenger for Wren."

"Don't." She looks down at the bandage on her finger. "Shit happens."

Shoving my credit card at her, I huff out a laugh. "You know it. Charge my mom's flowers to my card."

She waves it away with a flick of her hand. "Pay me when you pick them up. I haven't turned on the computer system yet since I don't officially open for business for another two hours."

"That's my cue to get the hell out of here, isn't it?" I ask half-teasingly.

"I don't want word getting around that I take orders before seven a.m.," she says, amusement lacing her tone. "I'll see you later, Liam."

That sets her off back toward the door of her store.

Once it's unlocked and she's pushed it open, I turn to face her. "Thanks again, Athena. Thanks for everything."

Her lips part in a soft smile. "I'm glad you stopped by."

I am too. I'm damn glad I stopped by.

# Chapter 6

### *Athena*

"Are you making that bouquet for the Queen of England?" Leanna squeezes my shoulder as she passes behind me. "It's taking you forever. It was perfect twenty minutes after you started."

I take a step back and survey the finished product. "Does it look like sunshine to you?"

"That face looks like sunshine to me." She circles a finger in front of me. "You've been grinning since I got here. What's that about?"

I point at the screen of the laptop Leanna set up on the corner of the table that we use as a workstation. The wooden table may be old, and the baby blue paint is chipping off of it, but it works for us. It belonged to the previous owner of the shop, so I've always considered it a good luck charm.

"Online orders have been coming in all day." I wink at her. "Why wouldn't I be grinning from ear-to-ear?"

Sliding her reading glasses up the bridge of her nose, she studies the screen of the laptop. "These orders are all from today?"

Nodding, I carefully place the vase containing the bouquet for Liam's mom into the cooler. I make a note of the order number on a piece of cardstock before tucking it between two yellow roses.

"They all came in since this morning." I stand next to her. "It's all thanks to you."

She tucks a lock of her black hair behind her ear. "I can't take credit for that. You need to thank Al. He's the one who came up with the design for that online ad."

My marketing efforts have been hit or miss. Jeremy Weston, my oldest brother, is always pitching new ideas to me. Most of them are fantastic, but some are better suited to selling vodka, not flowers.

Jeremy owns Rizon Vodka.

He understands that market. I have a pulse on this one. Together, we're learning what does and doesn't work when it comes to finding our niche in the oversaturated Manhattan florist scene.

When Al came to me with an idea for an online ad, I was skeptical, but once I saw the design and listened to Leanna's thoughts on our target market, it all made sense.

The steady stream of orders coming in today is proof of that.

"I'll take this one." Leanna taps her fingernail on the screen. "You're the daisy whisperer so that one is yours."

I toss my head back in laughter. "What does that even mean?"

"It means daisies aren't my favorite." She rolls her eyes. "Don't tell me that you haven't noticed."

"What did daisies ever do to you?"

"Al's second wife loved them," she scoffs. "He brought me a bouquet on our first date and told me as much."

Biting back a smile, I shake my head. "Bad Al."

"He's damn lucky I let that slide." She jerks a thumb over her shoulder toward the cooler. "You're on daisy duty. Hop to it, Boss Lady. These orders won't fill themselves."

***

Hours later, I finally set myself down on a wooden stool.

This is the first day in months that I haven't taken a lunch break. I made time for two bites of an apple. I kept hydrated with small sips from my water bottle every hour, but almost all of my focus was on flowers.

Leanna offered to stay past three, but I practically pushed her out the door.

Her mom lives in same building as she does, but I could tell that she was anxious to get home in time to greet her kids at the crosswalk in front of their school.

The ring of the bell over the shop door pulls me back to my feet.

I smooth my hand over my hair. I bunched it into a topknot mid-afternoon. No one who comes into Wild Lilac is focused on how I look. I don't want them to be. The flowers are the stars of the show.

"Hello again."

I turn at the sound of that voice. It's so deep and melodic.

Locking eyes with Liam Wolf, I smile. "Hi."

He traded in the jeans and T-shirt he was wearing earlier for a pair of charcoal gray pants and a black sweater.

Anything looks good on him.

The man is a sight for my very tired eyes.

He's invaded my thoughts throughout the day. I stole a glance at my phone from time-to-time waiting for a text from Liam to let me know when he'd stop by to pick up the bouquet he ordered. The two texts he sent me early this morning were straightforward. He apologized for unwittingly thrusting me into the middle of what he called '*an uncomfortable situation.*'

With a shake of my head, I snap back to the reality that I'm staring at a guy who had his heart crushed less than twenty-four hours ago.

"How did you make out with the sunshine bouquet?" His gaze trails over my shoulder to the coolers. "Tell me that's not the arrangement you made for my mom."

Without needing a peek, I know exactly what arrangement he's talking about. It's Leanna's handiwork. She prepared the centerpiece for a sunset wedding tomorrow. Al agreed to deliver it to the venue after he drops his wife off at work in the morning.

"You told me to dial it back." I laugh. "I listened."

I turn and walk toward the cooler. Sliding open one of the glass doors, I reach in and retrieve the small bouquet from the vase.

When I spin back around, Liam is right behind me. He's so close that the flowers brush against him.

"I'm sorry," I say, swatting a hand over his sweater even though the flowers didn't leave a trace of anything behind when they touched him. "I didn't know you were there."

His gaze drops to the bouquet in my hands. "That's for my mom?"

I hold it up proudly. "It's sunshine, right?"

He studies my face as a slow smile crawls over his lips. "I agree. It's pure sunshine."

Suddenly feeling as though I need air, I sidestep him. "I'll wrap these up."

I tug at the paper roll that's positioned at the end of the table. I chose a light purple paper for the shop. It fits the theme of the store.

Moving to the other side of the table, he crosses his arms. "How long have you been doing this?"

"I took over the store last year," I say. "But I've always loved floral design."

"You don't need me to tell you that you have talent." He laughs.

I'll take the compliment even if it's twisted in its wording. "Talent and training go a long way in this industry."

I'll never discount the training I've received over the years. I took night classes in floral design while I was earning a degree in business. My years spent working in flower shops gave me the foundation I needed to build a career of my own.

I point at the front counter. "You can fill out a card over there if you'd like. You'll find envelopes there too."

His gaze doesn't leave my face. "I'm good. There's no need for that."

I wrap the bouquet carefully before giving it to him. "We can settle up at the counter."

I hear his footsteps behind me as we make our way across the store.

Before I have a chance to show him the invoice, his credit card is in front of me. I run it through the register and hand it back to him. "Don't forget it this time."

He scoops up the card and shoves it in his pocket. "It looks like I'm all set."

I watch as he gingerly cradles the bouquet in his hand. For such a large man, I can tell he has a tender touch.

I dip my head down when I think of his hands on my skin.

I can't let my thoughts go there. He's a customer. His girlfriend just dumped him.

"Thanks again, Athena."

I glance up to find him looking at me. "It's my pleasure."

"Take care," he says in a low tone. "If I ever need flowers, I know just where to come."

I hope he needs flowers tomorrow, or the day after that.

As he exits the shop, I laugh off my eagerness to see him again.

This city is full of gorgeous men. I meet at least a few every week. I never think about them when they walk out of my store, but I know this time will be different.

Liam Wolf won't be as easy to forget.

# Chapter 7

### *Athena*

This is a daily habit I could get used to.

I smile at the man who walked into my store as I was about to lock the door for the day.

It was another busy one thanks to Al's brilliant marketing schemes. I had to bring in extra help today in the form of one of my weekend assistants. She's still in college but had a block of time free this afternoon. I put her to work, prepping the flowers that Leanna and I needed for the arrangements we had to get out before Al arrived to deliver them.

My great day just got better.

"Athena Millett." A smile tugs on the corners of Liam's mouth as he says my name. "I owe you."

I take in the sight of him as he strolls closer to where I'm standing in the middle of the store.

His hands are shoved into the front pockets of his dark blue pants. The light blue button-down shirt he's wearing is open at the collar and rolled at the sleeves. Today he's wearing brown oxfords on his feet.

*Damn, he's gorgeous.*

He rakes me from head-to-toe.

I tucked the front of my short-sleeved white sweater into black and white checkered pants. My low-heeled black boots are my most comfortable footwear, so they almost always make the cut when I'm getting dressed every morning.

As usual, I tied my hair up sometime around mid-morning when the mad rush started.

Pursing my lips, I ask the obvious question. "Why do you owe me?"

By the time the last word has left my mouth, he's in front of me. He smells as good as he looks. The scent of his cologne draws me a step closer to him.

"You made my mom cry."

I lift my chin to make eye contact with him. "The flowers made her cry? In a good way?"

Nodding, he looks around the store. "In the best way. Are you almost done here?"

"I'm never done here," I joke. "I was about to lock the door and call it a day."

"Have you had dinner yet?"

I blurt out the honest answer before I think it through "Not yet."

"Me either." He locks eyes with me. "Let me buy you dinner to repay you for making my mom happy."

"You made her happy by ordering the flowers," I point out. "I just arranged them in a bouquet. It's the thought that counts and that came from you."

"This wasn't the first time I gave her flowers." Stepping closer to me, he drops his tone. "She's never cried before."

I feel a twisted sense of pride in that. Not everyone has a visceral reaction to a bouquet, even if I hope they do. A lot of people only see flowers as a bright spot on a lousy day or a reminder of a birthday or an anniversary.

"Never?" I question with a tilt of my head.

"Never," he repeats. "So it stands to reason that I owe you. Dinner is on me if you're up to it."

I'm up to anything that keeps me this close to him for as long as possible.

He may have a broken heart beating inside that massively broad chest of his, but eating dinner with him can't hurt.

It's not a date. It's a *thank-you-for-being-a-great-florist* meal.

"Sure," I say simply. "I'll finish up and we can head out."

\*\*\*

Ordering salad was a mistake.

My stomach is still rumbling and now I'm worried that I have a piece of spinach stuck in my teeth.

I skim my tongue over the front of my top teeth. I don't feel anything, but a sip from the glass of water in front of me, along with a barely noticeable swish of it around my mouth, should dislodge anything green from between my perfectly straight teeth.

They are one of my best features.

I lucked out in the dental department. My mom's third husband wanted his stepchildren to be perfect. He slapped braces on my teeth along with my two younger brothers.

It was a gift that has kept on giving.

Liam watches me intently as he downs another half glass of water.

This dinner has been rated PG all the way including the cheeseburger and fries Liam ordered and our non-alcoholic beverages.

His attention has been on his phone as much as it's been on me. If this was a date, I might be offended, but he apologized every time it took his attention away.

I stole a glance at my phone once or twice too.

Seeing a steady stream of online orders coming in for tomorrow boosted my mood.

I'm going to head to the store an hour early in the morning. Sleep can wait when there are customers to keep happy.

"Are you a native New Yorker?"

This is a new direction for him. His first line of questioning while we waited for dinner was all about flowers. He politely asked how I know which blooms go with others.

I launched into a nervous speech about balance and beauty.

I'm sure I stopped making sense around the two-minute mark, but he just smiled and nodded.

Every time I thought of a question to ask him, his phone chirped and his gaze dropped to it.

"No," I answer succinctly not wanting to delve into the twisted tale of my childhood. "Are you?"

I'd rather fire off twenty questions at him about Wren, but I don't know him well enough to initiate a conversation about his personal life.

I've heard enough tales about breakups to last for the rest of my life. It's part of being a florist. People come into Wild Lilac all the time hoping that a handful of roses or a vase filled with daffodils will magically repair their broken relationship.

Maybe it works sometimes, but for the long term, it takes more than a few pretty flowers to fix a damaged bond.

"I was born and raised here." He chuckles. "It's home to me."

I lean back when a waiter buzzes past our table, picking up Liam's empty plate on his way. He twists his face in a scowl at the sight of my half-eaten salad.

I push it forward an inch in a silent offering to him, but he ignores me in favor of flashing a smile at Liam.

I can't blame him. Liam is the hottest guy in this place.

"I can't imagine living anywhere else." Liam hones in on a crumb in front of him. He swats it off the table with a push of his index finger. "What neighborhood is home to you?"

I tug on the corner of the paper napkin next to my water glass. "I live a few blocks from my shop."

I'd go on about how it's a modest studio apartment with a fireplace that doesn't work and a window seat that's as comfortable as it is cute, but those details only matter to me.

The apartment belonged to the former owner of Wild Lilac. She wanted to unload both in a package deal so she could retire in Arizona with no ties to New York. Jeremy negotiated a fair price. I expected him to turn around and sell the apartment after a few repairs, but he gave me the keys and told me to make him proud.

I've never lived alone before. I love it as much as I hate it.

Independence is everything. The loneliness is overwhelming at times, but I wouldn't trade those seven hundred square feet of my own space for anything.

"I live on the Lower East Side," he offers. "I've got a killer view of the East River."

*I've got a killer view right now.* Sitting across from him is better than any view in this city right now.

Another chime from his phone draws his gaze back to the screen.

This time he lets out a low chuckle. "My mom is still going on about the flowers. I'm officially her favorite son for the day. Thanks again for that, Athena. I appreciate it more than you know."

This seems like the perfect time to call it a night, so I do. "It was my pleasure and my job."

He laughs. "You're damn good at your job."

I push back from the table to see if he'll follow my lead. He does.

Standing, I glance down at my half-eaten salad. I'd take it to go, but I won't eat it.

"Thank you for dinner." I shoulder my navy blue tote.

He's on his feet too, sliding his phone into one of the front pockets of his pants. "You're welcome."

I wait for an offer to take me home or a promise that he'll see me soon, but silence fills the air between us.

"Take care, Liam."

His eyes find mine and for the briefest of moments I see a flicker of sadness. It makes sense given that his relationship ended just days ago.

"You too, Athena," he says softly. "Have a great night."

I sigh as I walk away. His heart needs time to mend and my body needs some relief after spending two hours staring at him.

"I will have a great night," I whisper as I exit the restaurant.

I head home knowing that before I fall asleep tonight I'll have a hot bath in my clawfoot tub and an orgasm courtesy of wicked thoughts of Liam Wolf.

# Chapter 8

*Liam*

"How's Wren?"

"Over me," I say matter-of-factly.

My oldest friend, Keats Morgan, huffs out a laugh. "What the fuck happened? I thought you two would make it to the finish line."

I rest my hands on the back of one of the armchairs in the middle of my office. "What's the finish line? Marriage? Kids?"

"Yes, and yes," he punctuates his answer with two nods of his chin. "You're the guy who said she had the potential to be *the one*. Correct me if I'm wrong, but those were your words, right?"

Sliding a palm over my forehead, I shake my head. "I never said that. Audrey is Wren's biggest fan. Maybe you got that from her?"

"You're probably right. Audrey does like to chat me up when I'm waiting for you." He crosses his arms. "So that's it? It's over between the two of you?"

"Don't sound so heartbroken, Keats." I chuckle. "This gives me more time to hang out with you."

His green eyes zero in on my face. "Is that a good thing?"

Keats and I have been through thick and thin. It started in preschool with a fistfight over a red crayon. Our parents were called down to sort it out. They hit it off. Joint birthday parties, family vacations, and life's ups and downs have cemented our bond.

Raking a hand through his black hair, he tosses me a look. "I need to get back to work. Thanks again for lunch, Wolf."

There it is, the nickname that has trailed me around forever.

My brothers, Nicholas and Sebastian, bestowed it on me when I was a baby because of the mane of hair on my head and my non-stop crying or howling as they refer to it.

Twenty-nine years later, they'll call me Liam on occasion, but my parents and sister still view me as Wolf. Keats does too.

Athena doesn't.

Damn, that woman left an impression on me.

Shaking her from my thoughts has been impossible since I last saw her. That was over a week ago.

Keats gives me a light slap on my cheek. "You're daydreaming, big guy."

I laugh. Keats is a few inches shorter than me, but he spends more time in the gym than I do. He always gives me a run for my money when we spar in the boxing ring.

"Is it about Wren?" he teasingly asks with a laugh. "Do you need your old buddy to talk to her? I can get her back in no time flat."

If there's a negotiation to be made, Keats is the man for the job. It's what he does for a living. He's an agent for a few of the biggest names in sports. He's good at it and I've told him as much.

"Wren is my past," I say it with conviction.

"Welcome back to single life." He throws an arm over my shoulder. "This requires a celebration. Does beer and pool on Friday work for you?"

"I'll be there." I point a finger at my office door. "Thanks for stopping by, but you need to get lost. I've got an appointment due to arrive any minute."

"I'm out." He tugs on the lapels of his gray suit jacket. "For what it's worth, I didn't think she was the right woman for you, Wolf."

Since this is the first I've heard of it, I press for more. "I thought you were team Wren. You two hit it off when we all hung out."

"I was drunk," he deadpans.

"You were sober," I counter.

"Drama followed Wren around like a lost puppy."

He's not wrong. In Wren's world, everything from a late client to a misplaced shoe was a catastrophe. I fielded calls and texts all day from her. I was the calming voice she needed. She was the distraction I wanted.

We worked until we didn't.

Two short rings of my office phone signal that my two o'clock appointment has arrived.

"That's my cue to fuck off." Keats heads toward the door. "I'll see you on Friday. Whoever loses two out of three games picks up the tab for the beers. Agreed?"

It's our standard set-up. More often than not, the drinks are on me.

Opening my office door, I nod. "Agreed. See you on Friday."

"If you need a shoulder to cry on before then, call someone else." He winks.

I laugh. "Go to hell."

"That's where I'm headed." He glances toward the waiting room. "I've got a meeting with a potential new client. Talk about drama. This guy gives Wren a run for her money."

"Good luck with that," I offer even though he won't need it.

"Same to you, Wolf."

His words hold more meaning than mine.

Counseling people through grief isn't easy, but it's what I was made for and what I'm good at.

Watching Keats breeze past the reception desk on his way out, my eye catches on a small bouquet of wilted flowers that Audrey brought in with her this morning. She said flowers brighten any space.

She's right. My apartment could use some brightening up and I know just how to make that happen.

# Chapter 9

### *Athena*

"What do you mean there's a request that I deliver an order?" I question Leanna.

The huge grin on her face is telling me that she knows exactly what's going on.

"You didn't set me up again, did you?" I manage a half-smile, even though my heart is racing inside my chest.

Leanna has taken on the role of my matchmaker.

I'm not on board for that.

I know she means well, but the two guys she already set me up with were not my type at all.

One was a lifeguard. He spent his summers in the Hamptons watching over the rich and famous. His winters weren't nearly as glamorous, and unfortunately, that's when we met for dinner.

I'm all for splitting the costs of dating, but he expected me to pay for his expensive dinner and the bottle of wine he finished on his own.

I didn't have a drop.

When he asked if he could borrow money to pay his cell phone bill so that he'd be able to text me the next day, I left the restaurant.

The second man that Leanna had in mind for me was a driving instructor. His sole goal during our two dates was to teach me how to drive even though I had no interest in it.

I spent four hours behind the wheel of his SUV with him breathing down my neck and not in a good way. By the time our second date was over, he had told me that I'd never cut it as his girl since I couldn't master a left turn.

I was fine with that. I don't need a driver's license or a man.

I do need an explanation for why I'm suddenly being thrust into delivery person mode by Leanna.

"Al can deliver that with the others when he picks you up." I glance at the clock on the wall. "I'll put the bouquet together now, so it will be good to go."

"Athena," she stresses with a tap of her fingernail on the laptop screen. "I don't think you understand. You need to deliver this order. The customer specifically requested you do it after seven tonight."

Without glancing at the order on the laptop screen, I shake my head. "As much as I appreciate you wanting to help me find a man, I'm not interested."

Her hand leaps to her mouth as she lets out a laugh. "When you told me to butt out of your personal life, Al said the same thing. I have nothing to do with this. I swear."

I lean in to get a better look at the order.

The customer's name is the same as the name for the delivery. *Liam Wolf.* I scan the address. It's on the Lower East Side. When we had dinner together, he told me he lived there.

He wants me to deliver flowers to his home? *Holy hell.*

I didn't expect to hear from him again. I thought the dinner was both a thank-you and a good-bye.

"Do you recognize the customer's name?" Leanna quizzes with a pop of her brows. "Is there something you'd like to tell me?"

Biting my bottom lip, I hold everything in. I can't tell if I'm more excited than nervous. "He's placed a couple of orders in the past."

Leanna studies my face. "There's more to this story than that."

Shrugging off her assumption, I point at the laptop screen. "I'll take care of that order. Why don't you get started on the one for Hunter Reynolds? He wants something special for his wife, Sadie, for their anniversary."

"I know what she likes," she says with confidence.

This is why I love having Leanna here. She has built up long-term relationships with many of the customers who have been coming to the shop for years.

"Tomorrow I expect to hear all the details about your delivery to Mr. Wolf on the Lower East Side."

I shoot her a look that's punctuated with a sly grin. "That falls under client and florist confidentiality."

Pointing a finger at me, she winks. "I knew something was going on. Good for you, Athena. Good for you."

Maybe at another time, he could be good for me, but I've never been a rebound, and I have no intention of stepping into that role now.

*** 

Red skinny jeans, a white sweater, my black leather jacket, and my favorite boots. That's what I'm wearing when I approach the address that Liam noted in his online order.

I considered going home to change my clothes, but I decided against it after looking in the full-length mirror hanging on the back of the door in the cramped office at Wild Lilac.

I smoothed my hair into a tight ponytail. After applying black eyeliner, mascara, and a sheer lip balm, I liked the way I looked.

Once I'm standing in front of the building, I realize that I have to be buzzed in.

Instead of pressing the button with *Wolf* written next to it, I send Liam a text message.

***Athena: I have a floral delivery for you.***

It doesn't take more than a few seconds for his reply to pop up on my phone.

***Liam: I'll buzz you in. Apartment 302.***

Swallowing past a lump of uncertainty that's lodged in my throat, I tug on the curved handle of the door once it buzzes.

Swinging it open, I strut through and head straight across the small lobby to an elevator.

The floors are polished marble in a decorative pattern that might have been popular decades ago. Worn woodwork lines the ceiling and a door labeled *custodian* is next to the elevator.

This building is full of charm, just like the one I live in.

Drawing in a shaky breath, I step into the elevator once the door slides open.

This is it. I'm about to come face-to-face with the man who has been on my mind for days.

A smile curves my lips as the narrow elevator starts upward with an unsteady lurch and a groan.

# Chapter 10

### *Liam*

There's something about this woman that sets me on fire whenever I'm near her.

I stand at the open door of my apartment and take it all in.

She's beautiful. It's not just Athena's face that is striking. It's everything about her.

The soft smile on her lips, the wisps of hair that are trailing across her cheek, and the subtle way she's tilting her head as she rakes me from head-to-toe make her hot as fuck in my eyes.

I had no idea if she'd show up with the bouquet.

I placed the order online this morning, hoping that she'd get a laugh out of it. I half-expected her to send someone else to put the flowers in my hand, but I'm glad she's here.

"You ordered a *surprise them* bouquet, so surprise," she says with a laugh.

I glance down at the small blue-hued bouquet that's sitting in a circular vase. Did she lug that here from her store? The woman is fearless if she took a breakable vase filled with water on a journey around Manhattan.

"I didn't realize it came with that," I point out, taking the flowers from her.

The vase has some weight to it.

"It doesn't," she says, edging a few inches to the left. "I didn't know if you'd have anything to put the flowers in, so I threw it in at no cost."

I owe her again.

*I'm a lucky bastard.*

I watch as her gaze flits from my face to the room behind me. She's checking out my apartment. It's not large, but it's comfortable.

A one-bedroom with a view of the river was what sold me on the place.

"Do you want to come in for a bit?"

She studies me, her brow knitting in concentration. I admit I didn't expect a pause, so I fill in the silence with a question. "Do you need to be somewhere else?"

A shake of her head confirms what I already suspected. "No."

"I don't have any alcohol to offer you, but I've got sparkling water."

A half-step forward and a nod of her chin are all I need. I step aside to let Athena into my home.

\*\*\*

I drape her leather jacket over the arm of the sofa as she stands at the windows that overlook the East River.

The small floral arrangement she brought with her has found its home on my reclaimed wood coffee table.

Athena took it from my hands when I stood in the center of the room silently debating where to place it.

I'm not a fresh flower kind of guy.

I've never lived with a woman, and since I'm not in the habit of ordering them for myself, flowers haven't played a part in the décor of this place.

My home is suited to me. It's simple and straightforward. The majority of my furniture is second-hand pieces I picked up in an antique shop an old friend owns.

I'll take comfort over design any day of the week.

When Athena placed the vase on the table, she tilted her head to the left and then the right. That sent her ponytail swinging.

I was spellbound as I watched her twist the vase one way a quarter of an inch until a satisfied smile set over her mouth.

Silently, I move into the kitchen and pour two tall glasses of chilled water.

I used to be a fridge full of beer kind of guy, but alcohol only works for me in moderation.

I reserve that indulgence for when I meet someone for a drink or when my brothers drop by with a case of the imported beer they think I love.

I don't.

It's out of my price range, so I let them believe what they will. I'm not going to turn down expensive beer if they're offering.

When I stroll back into the main living area, Athena's moved. She's standing in front of the sofa, staring at it like it's done her wrong.

A scowl mars her gorgeous face.

"Are you alright?" I ask because I know a pissed off look on a woman's face when I see it.

Skirting a hand over her brow, she sighs. "One of my suppliers is being a pain in the ass."

"Bastard."

Smiling, she looks down at her phone. "That's exactly what he is and he's proud of it."

"Something tells me you can handle him just fine."

With a half-shrug, she changes the subject. "You have a nice apartment."

I'll take the compliment and the opportunity to brighten her mood. "The flowers make all the difference. Feel free to use that as a new slogan for your store."

She chuckles. "I'll pass."

I push one of the glasses of water at her. "Do you have a slogan for your store?"

Taking a sip, she shakes her head. "I think the name speaks for itself."

I agree. It's what drew me inside when I ordered the bouquet for Wren.

I met my sister, Nikita, for a coffee that day and then set off on foot toward the nearest subway stop. I passed Athena's store on my way, and the name etched on the glass sparked something inside of me. I thought about Wren as I pulled on the door handle of Wild Lilac before I walked inside.

Now, I can't stop thinking about the woman standing in my apartment.

"Do you want to sit down?" I tug on the front of the gray T-shirt I'm wearing.

She looks at my shirt and faded jeans. My cock has been semi-hard since I opened the door and saw her. If she notices the bulge in my jeans, she's doing a hell of a good job hiding her reaction.

She lowers herself to the sofa, sliding her ass against the leather until she's teetering on the edge. I get that she's nervous as fuck right now. I am too. It's a first for me. I've had women here before, but this feels different.

I don't want to screw this up, so I take a deep breath and plant myself on the sofa too with some distance between us because I can tell she needs it.

She's got to wonder what the hell I'm doing ordering flowers and requesting that she deliver them.

"How old were you when you got your first tattoo?"

The question is so unexpected that I turn and stare at her. I catch her leaning forward, her gaze trailing over my arms.

"Fourteen," I admit.

"Fourteen?" she repeats back with a chuckle. "Isn't that illegal?"

"My oldest brother's friend knew a guy who knew a guy." I smile. "It was cash in the back room of his studio at night."

"Did you get in trouble?"

I like the innocence of the question. I appreciate that she's interested in my ink enough to ask. Most women give my arms a second look, but it doesn't go beyond that.

"It was here?" I pat my left shoulder. "I had to keep my shirt on at home for a few years."

"How long ago were you fourteen?"

"Fifteen years ago. You?"

"I'm twenty-three," she admits. "And I only have one tattoo. I got it last year on the day we launched Wild Lilac."

That catches me by surprise. "We?"

I'll take a step back if there's someone in the picture. This flirtation has been fun, but I respect the boundary of a committed relationship.

"My brother is my business partner."

Since we're circling the question, I go ahead and ask it for clarity. "Are you involved with anyone, Athena?"

Her mouth pops open to form a sexy little '*O.*'

"You already know that I'm not," I offer to pave the way. "I'm curious about you."

Hesitation swims in her eyes. I doubt like hell I misread the sparks that have been flying between us since the night we met. If she's taken, I'll back off, but I want to know.

Her gaze drops before it settles back on my face. "You and Wren just broke up."

"I'm aware," I answer curtly. "My question wasn't about her. It was about you."

"I know." Pushing to her feet, Athena glances over when I do the same. For a brief second our eyes meet and there's no way in hell that she doesn't feel the energy between us.

I lay my cards on the table before she can grab her jacket and head out of my apartment. "I'm not looking for anything serious. I like you. I'm attracted to you. I want to take you to dinner again."

She mulls my words with a tap of her boot against the floor. "I don't know, Liam."

"We'll have dinner," I say. "We'll hang out and see where it goes. No expectations."

Silence swims in the air between us.

"I just got out of a relationship," I point out. "I'm not looking to get into another if that's what you're worried about."

Relief softens her stance. I see it in the way the corners of her mouth quirk up toward a smile. "We'll keep it casual?"

It's what I need. It's exactly what I want, so I nod a little too vigorously. "I'm not looking for more."

With a bite of her bottom lip, she tilts her chin up. "I'm free next Wednesday if that works for you."

I'll damn well make it work. "I'll drop by the store at seven to pick you up."

She reaches for her jacket. "I'll see you then, Liam."

Walking her to the door I realize that I won't see her again until next week. I'll use the time to calm the fuck down, so when I do pick her up, my body won't be thrumming with the same need it is now.

# Chapter 11

### *Athena*

Agreeing to have dinner with Liam was a bad idea.

I knew that as soon as I left his apartment, but I promised myself that I'd give it a day or two before I sent him a text telling him that I changed my mind.

That day or two morphed into an entire week.

Now, I'm sitting across from him in a crowded restaurant while he tries to get rid of a woman who approached us as soon as we sat down.

I'm no expert on spotting former lovers, but the way she licked her lips when she saw him and tousled her brown hair, made it crystal clear that they're more than casual acquaintances.

"I thought you were dating someone named Robin." The woman eyes me up.

"Wren," Liam corrects her with a glance at me. "That's over now."

I reach over to the basket in the middle of the table filled with warmish breadsticks. The waiter plopped it down before he took our drink orders.

It was water for both of us again.

We're sitting in a massive seafood restaurant in the heart of Times Square. It gets high marks from tourists and New Yorkers alike because it's part of a nationwide chain. You know exactly what you'll get when you walk through the doors.

I admit I love shrimp and lobster as much as the next person. I've just never been to a place where someone dressed in a pirate costume delivers it to the table.

I hear someone shouting, "*Ahoy Matey*" in the distance.

"So Athena." The woman enamored with Liam enunciates each syllable of my name with a tick of her finger in the air. "How long have you two been friendly?"

Taking a bite of the breadstick, I defer that question to Liam with a lift of my brows.

"If you'll excuse us, Darcy." Liam shifts in his chair so he's facing me directly. "Athena and I were in the middle of a conversation."

We weren't, but I appreciate his effort to get her to scram.

Darcy shoots me the same look that she gave me when Liam first introduced us. He fumbled over what to call me, so I interjected and called myself his friend as I offered her my hand.

Manners matter, after all.

"If you need anything, I'm here for you." Darcy juts her chest out. Her tits are already straining against the tight white T-shirt she's wearing.

It would be my luck that Liam's former lover opted to wear black leather pants the same night that I did.

Her T-shirt is winning the battle over my black sweater mostly because I'm wearing a bra, and Darcy clearly isn't.

The air conditioning in this place is working to her advantage.

Liam doesn't take the bait. He keeps his gaze leveled on my face.

"Well, bye for now, Liam?" Her hands drop to her hips.

*Is that a question?*

He waves a hand over his shoulder without looking at her.

As she saunters away, shaking her ass, I break out a smile. "She seems nice."

Laughing, he glances around. "Would you be upset if we got out of here? I know you like the food at this place, but…"

"I like the food at this place?" I shake my head. "I don't. I've never been here before."

"You order take-out from here though."

He has me confused with someone else, with another woman.

Humiliation creeps over me, flushing my cheeks with a pink hue.

"When I threw the broken glass from the vase in the trash at Wild Lilac, I saw a cardboard container in there with the name of this place stamped on it." He glances at a group of pirates singing Happy Birthday to a woman wearing a tiara. "And their take-out menu was sitting on the counter when I paid for my mom's flowers."

*Leanna.*

She's always ordering something for lunch. I've never taken her up on her offer to share because I know that Al loves the leftovers.

"Someone I work with has been ordering food from here." I watch as the woman in the tiara stands to give a speech.

"Dammit." Liam rests both elbows on the table. "I'll never cut it as a detective."

I'm touched that he took the clues he found at my shop and ran with them.

"What are you in the mood for?" he asks just as his phone starts up on a ring.

His gaze cuts to where it's sitting on the table. His hand reaches out once he sees the name that's popped up on the screen.

"I have to take this." Shooting me an apologetic look, he brings the phone to his ear.

I'd excuse myself to give him privacy, but he's on his feet headed straight for the exit before I can say a word.

*** 

When Liam pushes the sleeves of his sweater up to his forearms, my gaze drifts over the shaded ink that covers his skin.

"Tell me about your tattoo, Athena."

I didn't think he would remember. I thought when I mentioned it last week that it had gotten lost in the moment.

Twirling around, I lift my hair to show him the back of my neck. "It's there."

I feel his breath graze over the exposed skin. It sends a shiver through me straight to my core.

"It's a flower," he whispers. "What is that? A lilac?"

I stay in place too long, my hair bunched in my hand, my heart twisting in my chest, and the spot between my legs aching.

"One lilac," I say quietly into the night air.

"It's beautiful."

I close my eyes, willing him to reach out to run a fingertip over it, but I sense the second he pulls back.

My hair falls from my hand as I spin back around to face him.

"I'm sorry again for what happened at the restaurant."

It's the second apology he's offered since we left Times Square. A client had called him. It was someone who had lost a spouse. They needed a few minutes of Liam's time to get them through the hours until they could see him in his office tomorrow.

I've suffered loss in my life but not that final.

The person I lost is sitting in a jail cell upstate. She's rotting away because she chose a man and money over everything else. The price my mother paid for her pursuit of happiness cost her a future with my brothers and me.

"Where should we eat?" He looks around at the shops that are shuttered and the restaurants that are boasting lines of diners waiting patiently for a table. A couple brushes past us with a pizza box in their hands.

I make a suggestion I hope I won't regret. "We could pick up a pizza to go."

"To go?" His left brow arches in surprise. "Back to your place or mine?"

I'm not ready to take him home with me yet, so I opt for the closer choice. "Your place isn't far from here. Let's go there."

Staring at me, a smile ghosts his mouth. "Pizza at my place? I'm in."

# Chapter 12

## *Liam*

After throwing the paper napkin in my hand into the center of the empty cardboard pizza box, I rub my stomach through my sweater. "That was good."

Athena pitches her napkin at the box too, but it sails right over. Once it's landed on the floor, she rolls her eyes. "Ignore that."

Reaching for it, I huff out a laugh. "I didn't see that. Give it another try."

Balling the napkin tighter, she launches it again. This time it twists over itself in the air before it lands squarely on the lid of the box.

"She shoots, she scores." I pump a fist in the air. "That's two points for Millett."

Shaking her ass on the sofa, she waves both hands in the air. "Hell yeah."

This feels so damn good.

I could tell she was nervous after we ordered the pizza and waited for it. Her gaze kept volleying past me to the door. I thought she was planning to make a break for it, but she hung around.

We walked back to my apartment talking about food.

She loves toasted sourdough bread with cream cheese and berries. When she asked me about my favorite food, I went with an easy answer.

Pizza.

I eat to fuel my body. I try to avoid the junk food aisles at the grocery store, but I'm human. A man can't survive on fruits, vegetables, and protein alone.

With a heavy swallow, I finish the water in my glass.

I turn to find Athena's eyes glued to me.

Tossing her a smile, I pick up her empty glass. "Do you want a refill?"

She looks at her phone's screen. It's the second time she's checked it since we sat down to eat.

I silenced mine because I stopped being on call fifteen minutes ago. If an emergency call comes into the Dehaven Center tonight, the phone service knows to contact Winola Dehaven, the founder and my boss.

If she doesn't pick up, they'll reach out to one of the other three counselors I work with.

"I should go soon." Her voice takes on the same nervous edge it had back at the restaurant. "I have a busy day tomorrow."

I do too, but it's early. "Can you stay for a few more minutes? I think I have a candy bar in the drawer. We can share it for dessert."

She shifts so she's facing me. "How long has it been in the drawer?"

Good question. I bought it for my niece, Winter, when I was hanging out with her one day. "Six months. A year tops."

Reaching for her purse, she scrunches her nose. "I bought one yesterday. Let's stay safe and share that."

Pausing, I watch her every move. She tugs the bag onto her lap before her hand disappears inside it.

"I know I didn't eat it," she whispers. "It has to be in here."

Holding the bag open, she searches through it. "How can a candy bar disappear just like that?"

I inch closer to get a better look. The bag is filled with everything I'd expect it to be. A package of tissues, a set of keys, and a black leather wallet are the first things I spot.

"I found it," she announces, yanking her hand swiftly out in triumph.

The candy bar appears along with something else.

A foil packet bounces off her lap before settling on the sofa between us.

"That wasn't supposed to happen," she says with a stuttered laugh.

Before she has a finger on it, I've got the package in my hand. I close my fist around it.

"That's mine." The words come out breathless. "Liam, that's mine."

"You won't need it tonight." I toss the package over my shoulder.

Her eyes follow the movement of my hand. "I didn't put that condom in my bag tonight. It's been in there for months."

Nodding, I take in the flustered look on her face.

"For the record, I didn't plan on having sex with you tonight. I wasn't going to have sex with you tonight."

I lean forward, enjoying the way her cheeks have flushed pink. "For the record, Athena, that condom wouldn't fit. I buy a specific brand. Size extra large."

Her reaction says it all. Her lips part, her breathing stalls, and her gaze drops to my lap.

I may be only semi-hard at the moment, but the bulge in my jeans is enough to send Athena to her feet.

Silently, she rounds the coffee table in search of the condom I tossed.

I stand too, raking a hand through my hair. "Let's say we split that candy bar now."

"No." Her voice comes out shaky. "I should go. It's larger than normal."

*She has no fucking idea.*

Biting back a laugh, I clear my throat. I'll drop my jeans right now and show her, but I sense the condom remark was enough for tonight.

"I meant that my delivery is larger than normal." She scoops up the condom and tucks it into her pocket. "It's arriving extra early in the morning, so I should go and get some sleep."

I can't argue with that logic. I respect her work. I won't get in the way of that.

"I'll take you home," I offer.

"No," she says with a scrub of her hand over the back of her neck. Her fingers skirt right over that sexy tattoo she has. "I'll be fine. You stay here."

Nodding, I take a step closer to her. "I'll see you again soon?"

"I have plans this weekend, so maybe one night next week?" She reaches for her purse and her phone. "We can touch base on Monday to see what works."

"Monday it is."

"Thanks for the pizza." She sets off toward my apartment door. "I had fun."

I did too, although it wasn't the type of fun I anticipated when I picked her up from Wild Lilac hours ago. I haven't had a date that didn't end in at least a kiss in years. I'm aching to touch her, but I'm fine with her setting the pace.

Swinging open the door, she takes a step out. "One last thing, Liam."

I stalk toward her, hoping that whatever it is, it involves my mouth on her body. "What's that?"

Her hand lands in the middle of my chest. With her thickly lashed blue eyes pinned to my face, she smiles. "That bouquet needs fresh water. You should change it out."

Reaching down, I scoop her hand into mine.

She tries to tug it away, but I hold tight. When I bring it to my lips, she lets out the smallest moan.

Pressing a kiss to the top of her hand, I lock eyes with her. "I'll do that before I fall asleep tonight. That and more."

A knowing smile tugs at the corners of her mouth. "Goodnight, Liam."

"Goodnight, Athena."

# Chapter 13

### *Athena*

I can't believe Liam Wolf tossed out the fact that he uses extra large condoms like it's no big deal.

That's intimate information. It's private.

I don't go around telling people that my bra size is 32B.

I'm small enough that I can get away without wearing a bra but big enough that I have curves that I like.

My breasts are my business unless I invite you to get better acquainted with them.

Men are different. I think that their cocks are directly attached to their egos.

The first time I realized it was in high school during gym class. Some guys wore shorts that were tight enough that I could have guessed the size of condoms they'd need.

None of those were extra large.

The size of Liam's package doesn't intimidate me. The undeniable attraction I feel for him does.

Last night was fun. I felt comfortable and at ease.

I liked it.

I like him.

The sound of the bell ringing over Wild Lilac's door shatters my daydream about Liam. I move to stand, but as soon as I notice Leanna's hand waving in the air, I sit back down.

I'm tired. I didn't get into bed until after midnight. I snuck in three hours of restless sleep before I got up, showered, dressed, and walked over to the shop.

The delivery wasn't scheduled until five, but I felt my creative juices flowing, so I sat at the table with my sketchpad and crafted a rough drawing of an arrangement that I'll offer on the website as a special for this month.

If I give my customers what they want, they'll keep coming back for more.

It's a proven business principle that hasn't failed me yet.

"Guess what I brought you?" Leanna waves a pizza box in the air. "Breakfast."

I stifle a laugh. "You brought me pizza for breakfast?"

"You know you want to eat it." Flapping the lid open and shut, she shows me a fleeting glimpse of what looks like a fully loaded medium pizza.

"You didn't eat any of that?"

Setting the box on the table in front of me, she narrows her eyes. "I was too excited to eat."

If she's pregnant, I'll cry both happy and sad tears. I desperately need her as much as she desperately wants to have another baby.

My gaze drops to the front of the faded jeans she's wearing. We're twinning today in our jeans and black T-shirts.

Her hand falls to her stomach. "I am not with child."

I laugh at the formality in her tone. "You're not?"

"I'm with a woman who is keeping a big secret." Her pointer finger lands on the tip of my nose.

I inch back until her hand drops. "I have a big secret?"

Sliding a piece of pizza from the box, she takes a huge bite. "Does this pizza smell familiar to you?"

I'd say that pizza is pizza, but I suspect that would offend her. Leanna is a foodie. She loves to eat and she knows where to get the best of everything in this city.

Eyeing the box, I shrug my shoulders. "It smells like good pizza?"

"It's the best pizza in Manhattan," she corrects me.

I'll take her word for it. Inching forward, I steal another peek inside the box. I only ate a banana this morning before I left my apartment. My stomach has been growling with hunger ever since.

"Al picked this up on his way home last night." She goes for another slice. "He ordered a large pepperoni and mushroom for the kids to share with him. I'm a fan of this all veggie pie."

I don't care what's on it; my mouth is now officially watering.

"You ordered a large margherita."

My hand drops right before I grab a slice. "I what?"

How does she know what kind of pizza I had last night? When Liam asked what I wanted, I went with my favorite.

"Or rather, your date ordered the large margherita."

I swallow past the unexpected lump in my throat.

"Al didn't want to interrupt." She slides the box closer to me. "He said you two looked cozy."

"We just met," I explain. "I haven't known him long enough to get cozy with him."

"Longish hair, a beard, muscles in all the right places, and tattoos." She fans herself. "Even Al said he was hot. You need to get cozy with that now."

Laughing, I take a bite of the cold but delicious pizza. "His girlfriend dumped him not long ago."

"His ex-girlfriend, you mean," she corrects me. "If that mattered to him, he would have been eating pizza in bed with her last night."

"We didn't eat it in bed." I chew on the crust.

"You ate it and then went to bed?" she asks hopefully. "Tell me you saw that unclothed, Athena."

I shake my head. "No. His break up is still fresh. It's too soon."

Wiping the back of her hand across her mouth, she winks. "It's never too soon for really good sex."

"Who said anything about it being really good?"

"Al snapped a picture of you and the pizza man." She bats her eyelashes. "A man that looks that good can't be bad in bed. There's a universal law against it."

I almost choke on the pizza. "There's not."

Wagging a finger at me, she laughs. "Prove me wrong. Sleep with him."

We both turn when the bell rings over the shop's door.

Leanna rubs her palms together shaking off a few crumbs. "I'll take care of whoever that is. You finish your breakfast and think about what I said."

I'll think about it. The truth is that I haven't stopped thinking about Liam and his extra-large condoms since I left his apartment last night.

# Chapter 14

### *Liam*

It's seven p.m. on Monday, and I've lost track of how many times I've checked my phone today.

What the hell is it about Athena that has me wound up this tight?

I started my day off right with a decaffeinated coffee and a good morning text to the owner of Wild Lilac.

That was twelve hours ago. I looked at my damn phone every chance I could, but my text is still unanswered.

If I weren't sitting across from a man who lost his mother three weeks ago, I'd be typing out another message to the woman I was hoping I'd see before the end of the day.

It doesn't look like that's going to happen.

"Is your mom alive, Wolf?"

I try to keep my own experiences out of my sessions, but sometimes it's necessary to share. I nod my head. "Yes."

"That makes me hate you."

It's the first sign of a smile I've seen on his face. Rhys Quillan is nineteen. He's still living in a world where his parents fill in the gaps in his life. He's a first-year student at NYU but he lives at home in a four-storey, brownstone that overlooks Central Park with a staff of five people and a father who hasn't said a word since his wife died.

Deidre Quillan was everything to her husband and son.

Cancer didn't give a shit.

"I understand," I offer. "You hate your circumstance."

Nodding, he glances at the door. "People around me tell me that it will get easier, but I don't see it. How? How the fuck does it get easier?"

"Time." I point a finger at him. "I know you think that's bullshit, Rhys, but it helps. It doesn't erase the pain, but you'll process this. If day-by-day feels like too much, look at it as hour-by-hour or minute-by-minute."

"I'm dragging my dad down here next week." He tugs on the arm of the black sweatshirt he's wearing. "You'll talk to him, too, right?"

Seeing as how his mom took the unusual step of coming to see me when she was first diagnosed with stage four brain cancer six months ago, I'll do whatever I can.

Deidre wanted her boys (*as she called them*) to be taken care of. She pre-paid for more than a year's worth of sessions for Rhys and his dad.

Rhys took the advice she left him in her goodbye note.

He was sitting across from me the day after her funeral. His dad is a harder sell. He'll get here, if and when he's ready.

I lean forward, resting my elbows on my thighs. "You know if it works for him, we can meet at the park two blocks from here. He's got some skills on the basketball court, right?"

Rhys's mom painted a picture of her husband that was so vivid that I already feel as though I know him.

"You'd do that?" Rhys's pierced brow pops. "You're a little taller than him. You'd blow him away."

Resting back in my chair, I flick a piece of lint off my black pants. "Mention the idea to him and see what he thinks."

"My time is up," he says with a hint of resignation in his tone. "I'll take off."

Rising to my feet, I offer him a hand. He takes it, pulling himself up.

"This was good, Wolf," he says quietly. "I'm glad I came."

"Me too, Rhys." I pat him on the shoulder as he walks to the door. "Call me anytime."

The pain he's in his palpable. I'll do my best to help ease that, but he needs to do the heavy lifting. He made a step in the right direction today.

***

Just as I round the corner headed to my apartment building, my phone buzzes with a notification of a new text message.

Like a high school kid with a permanent hard-on for the new girl in class, I whip my phone out of my pocket in record time.

"Finally," I mutter under my breath, followed by a laugh.

I don't instant text anyone. If you send me a text message, give me an hour or two to respond before you start giving me shit for ignoring you.

My family is on board with that. My friends get it. The women I've dated in the past learn to live with it.

I won't debate the importance of carrying our lives around in our pockets, but everyone needs a breather from their device.

I try to give myself at least an hour a day for that. It's more if I've been pulled through the wringer at work.

I read the text message I've been waiting all day for.

**Athena: Good evening. I can't say good morning because it's way past morning. Where did the day go?**

I respond because I want to know more, about her day, and her.

**Liam: Where are you now?**
*Way to pace yourself, Wolf.*

I wait for her to answer, but when a minute passes with nothing, I head up to my apartment.

Once I'm inside, I rid myself of the button-down shirt I've been wearing all day. My belt hits the floor too before my pants, socks, and shoes follow.

I adjust my dick inside my black boxer briefs.

That semi hard-on problem is back in full force.

Just thinking about Athena is all it takes.

**Athena: I'm at the shop. I have a private consult at 8 for a 50th birthday party next month.**

As much as I'd like to see her tonight, I'm beat and she's busy.

**Liam: *Do you want to catch a movie one night this week?***

I haven't been to the movies in years, but there's something alluring about the idea of sitting next to Athena in a darkened theater.

Her response isn't immediate. I wait with my phone in my hand, tapping my toes on the floor.

I need to shower and eat.

I should toss my phone on the sofa and get back to my life.

**Athena: *Later in the week works for me. I have a drop-in class tomorrow and another one on Thursday. Flower arranging classes here at the shop so I'm busy.***

I'm pulling the evening shift on Wednesday, so I move to firm up Friday now.

**Liam: *Let's do Friday.***

**Athena: *Friday is good. Pick me up at 8 at Wild Lilac?***

Typing out my response, I smile like a fucking idiot.

**Liam: *I'll see you at Wild Lilac.***

Tomorrow. I don't add that to the text, but that's my plan. I'm all for learning new skills. Flower arranging may come in handy someday.

# Chapter 15

*Athena*

Trying to teach a basic floral arranging class while Liam Wolf is in the building is almost impossible.

Most of the people who showed up for this fifty dollar, *you-take-your-bouquet-home* class are my regular customers. I don't know if they dropped in because they felt pressured by all the times I've mentioned it over the last month, or if they see themselves as potential future employees of Wild Lilac.

I'd love to hire another designer, but I need more money coming in. That's one of the reasons I decided to offer these classes. The other is because I want to connect more with my clientele.

My clientele wants to connect with Liam.

I don't think anyone has heard a word I've said. Maybe Liam has. He's been staring at me since he got here.

I'm glad I cleaned myself up after work. I went home, took a shower, straightened my hair, and put on black yoga pants and a white T-shirt with Wild Lilac stitched across the front of it in dark purple thread.

The shirts are another idea straight from Al.

Leanna gave me one this morning. I thought the class tonight would be the right time to debut it.

"How about we take a break?" I announce so that the seven women in attendance can catch their breath.

Staring at a gorgeous man in a black T-shirt and jeans is hard work.

Liam steps toward me, but he's cut off by two women who jump in front of him to compliment him on the arrangement he's been working on.

"Who is he?"

A familiar voice lures my gaze to the left. Mrs. Ducat, one of the sweetest people I've ever met, is standing next to me.

She picks up a dozen pink roses every Wednesday morning like clockwork.

"A friend," I say with a sigh.

"Boyfriend?" she asks, reaching to tug my hand into hers.

I look down at her weathered skin. Her touch is gentle, just as I suspected it would be. She's a grandmother to ten and a great-grandma to one. I never knew my grandma. I wish I had.

"No," I correct her with a smile. "He's just a friend."

"I never had a friend that looked like that." Her brow twitches. "He's something, Athena."

He is. I can't argue with her.

A change of subject is in order, so I point at the arrangement that Mrs. Ducat put together. "You did a wonderful job on that."

With a cluck of her tongue, she squeezes my hand. "We both know you're the one with the magic touch. Your talent is rare. Never stop what you're doing."

I take the compliment with an appreciative nod. "I won't. This is what I do best."

\*\*\*

"This is for you." Liam shoves the bouquet he crafted during class into my hands.

I smile because as sweet as the gesture is, his floral arranging skills aren't on point. That wasn't for lack of trying. He listened intently to my instructions, but he was distracted so often by his classmates talking to him, that his arrangement didn't turn out close to the way it should have.

He wasn't the only one with a less than stellar end product.

Most of the women who were here left with bouquets that looked like they were put together in the dark. Mrs. Ducat's was the exception. She walked away with a beautiful bunch of flowers in her hand.

"Thank you." I nestle the arrangement in the crook of my arm. "I didn't expect to see you here tonight."

He settles back on the heels of his boots. "A man should never stop learning. Today it was flower arranging. Tomorrow it'll be something else. On a scale of one-to-ten, how did I do?"

"Five-and-a-half," I answer matter-of-factly. "For a first try, not bad."

He huffs out a laugh. "Not bad? That's all you've got?"

I shrug. "What can I say? I've seen better and I've seen worse."

"You're doing this again on Thursday?"

I won't complain if he wants to drop in again. I know my other students won't either.

"If I didn't have to work, I'd be back here inching my way closer to a ten."

Disappointment stalls in my chest. I shouldn't feel that. We're barely acquaintances. We've spent all of our time dancing around our mutual attraction.

I breathe in a sigh when I think about the condoms that are undoubtedly tucked into a drawer in his bedroom.

"Do you want to come back to my place?" he tosses the question out with ease.

I'm not ready for the extra large condoms, so I shake my head. "I can't tonight. I have to clean up here and then I'm meeting someone."

He rakes me over. I look like I'm on my way to yoga class. "For a drink?"

"Yes."

Technically it's a drink. I'm having coffee with my sister-in-law, Linny. She asked me to stop by after this class so we can catch up. We used to spend an hour every morning chatting over breakfast, but since I've moved out, we've been relying on text messages to stay connected.

Tonight is the first chance we've had to hang out in weeks.

"Are we still on for Friday?" he quizzes with a half-smile.

"Friday at eight."

"I'm looking forward to it." He bends his knees until his face is level with mine. "Thanks for teaching me a thing or two tonight, Athena. I hope I can do the same for you very soon."

I stare at his mouth. His top lip dips into a soft curve in the middle. His bottom lip is plump and a shade of pale pink that's almost too perfect. I imagine the sound he must make when a woman's teeth latch onto it.

My teeth. My mouth. On his.

Leaning forward, he brushes those lips over my cheek. His breath is warm and scented with mint. "Until Friday, Athena."

My fingers trail over my cheek when he leaves.

"Until Friday," I whisper, wishing I had the super power to speed up time.

# Chapter 16

### *Liam*

"You chose that movie because you look like the main character," Athena accuses through a grin. "Just admit it, Liam."

It's not the first time someone has told me that I resemble Aquaman. I see it. My hair is a few shades lighter, my beard is shorter, but there's a similarity that I can't deny.

"I can't swim," I admit on a heavy sigh.

My attempt to change the subject works. Athena lets out a stuttered laugh. "You can't swim?"

Crossing my arms over my chest, I paste on the best scowl I can muster. "Are you seriously laughing at me right now?"

My weak attempt to look pissed doesn't faze her. "I'm not laughing at you. I'm laughing with you."

Taking a step toward her, I tilt my chin up. "I'm not laughing, lilac."

The nickname stops her cold. Her plump lips part before they curve up into a smile. "You want to laugh."

I want to kiss her. I've been fucking thinking about kissing her since I picked her up at her shop.

Her long hair flew over her shoulder when she turned around and saw me. She was dressed all in white. She looked incredible in skinny jeans and a short-sleeve sweater. She topped that with her black leather jacket when we left the store.

She's the most effortlessly beautiful person I've ever met.

I hold steady with my commitment not to crack a smile. "Can you swim?"

Sucking her cheeks in, she purses her lips. "Like a fish."

I can't contain the laugh that escapes me. "That's a great look for you."

"Try it." Her finger circles the air in front of my mouth. "Do fish lips for me."

"Fish lips?" I question back as if I have no fucking idea what she's talking about.

Fish lips are Winter's favorite thing at the moment. She's been trying to teach her younger sister how to master the move. She learned it from me.

My contributions as an uncle go above and beyond taking toys and candies to my nieces.

"Like this?" Athena sucks her cheeks in again. "You try."

I don't know why the hell we're doing this right outside the theater, but I'm on board for whatever this woman wants.

The corners of my lips twitch. "Show me again."

She does. She tilts her head to the left and the right as she purses her lips out.

I lean in, breathing a path over her cheek. "I think I need a closer look."

She keeps it up, sucking in her cheeks and wiggling her lips.

When I'm less than an inch from her, I mimic the movement of her mouth with mine.

She leans back, taking it in.

I have to look like a goddamn fool, but I don't give a shit.

"You're good at that," she whispers. "Really good."

"I'm better at this," I say before I tangle my hand in the hair on the back of her head and finally take her sweet mouth in a kiss.

\*\*\*

I wrap an arm around her tiny body and tug her closer, my lips still on hers, our tongues sliding against each other.

I don't care that people are passing by us. Let them stare. This feels too good, too natural for me to want to stop anytime soon.

A small moan escapes her before she steps back, pushing her hands against my chest with little effort. "Liam."

My knees buckle at the sound of the desire wrapped up in that one word.

*Jesus.* What the fuck would it sound like to hear her scream my name when I'm balls deep inside of her?

"Athena," I say her name quietly. "Come home with me."

I don't want to fight what I'm feeling anymore. I want her. I'm hard as nails right now, and I know the instant I taste her skin, I'll be close to losing it.

I haven't felt this desperate for a woman's touch before. I'm craving it more than my next breath.

"I'm not sure…" Her voice trails as hesitancy flashes across her face.

"We can just kiss," I spit out like I'm a horny fourteen-year-old kid who will do anything to be near the girl he's crushing on. "Whatever you're comfortable with. Nothing more."

Relief pulls the corners of her lips up. "You're sure?"

Hell no, but I've never pushed a woman to do more than she's ready for. I sure as fuck won't start tonight.

If all I get is another taste of that perfect mouth, I'll fall asleep happy.

"I can come over for a little while." Her hand slides into mine.

I'll take whatever time she'll give me because I'm already addicted to her. I keep that to myself. Squeezing her hand in mine, I kiss her again. This time it ends with a scrape of her teeth over my bottom lip.

I swear to God I could blow a load just from that.

Sucking in a deep breath, I tug on her hand. "Let's go, lilac."

# Chapter 17

## *Athena*

It takes a fool to know one.

I know one. I'm staring at her in the mirror in Liam Wolf's bathroom.

I'm second-guessing my decision to come here.

"Get it together, Athena," I whisper harshly to myself. "You can do this."

I haven't decided what exactly '*this*' is yet. After kissing Liam, I want more. How could I not?

His kiss did things to me. It made me imagine being underneath him and orgasms brought on by something other than my hand or one of the toys I keep hidden in my bedside table.

I haven't had the best luck with my past lovers.

There are only two of them. I thought the first was all right until I got into bed with the second a year later and realized that sex could be kind of good.

Liam's kiss was better than anything I did with either of those men.

A rush of air escapes my lungs as I hear Liam's footsteps on the hardwood floor in the hallway outside the door.

"Athena?" His gravelly voice rumbles through the locked door. "Are you okay?"

*No. I'm freaking the fuck out right now.*

"I'm fine," I call back. "I'll be out in two minutes."

Or ten; maybe twenty at the most.

"Take your time." His tone deepens. "I put on some music. Join in if you catch me dancing."

I smile to myself. I should jump into this with everything that I have, but I'm scared. I admit it. I'm afraid because he's too good to be true and I'm terrified because he just got dumped.

I rest my head against the door when I hear him pad away on bare feet.

He took off the boots he was wearing as soon as we got here. I did the same. I dropped my coat on his sofa before I asked where the washroom was.

I needed some air and a chance to catch my breath after the kiss.

*That kiss.*

Turning to the mirror again, I point a finger at my reflection. "Don't overthink this."

It's my mantra. When you grow up in the shadow of uncertainty around every corner, you learn how important a well thought out plan is.

Meeting Liam wasn't part of my plan. Standing in his apartment with bare feet and a racing pulse wasn't either.

The faint sound of music playing lures my hand to the doorknob.

I twist the lock, turn the handle, and swing it open.

Tonight isn't about a plan. Tonight is about having an adventure. I'm ready for whatever it is.

\*\*\*

He's not dancing when I walk back into the main living space. He's picking at the bouquet that is sitting in the middle of his coffee table.

Petals fall to the wood as he tries to adjust the browned bits of the blossoms.

Those flowers are past their due date.

"You didn't change the water when I told you to," I accuse trying not to laugh.

He peers over his shoulder at where I'm standing. "Are you saying that was a direct order? I took it as more of a suggestion."

Dropping my hands to my hips, I shake my head. Adding in a sigh for good measure, I tap my foot on the floor. "You killed those flowers, Liam."

That spins him around until he's facing me.

*Holy fuck.*

His hair is a mess in a very good, very sexy way. He's unbuttoned the top two buttons of the black shirt he's wearing, and he's rolled the sleeves up to his elbows.

"You'll forgive me, right?"

Tapping my fingertip against my chin, I ponder the question with a bat of my eyelashes. "I don't know that I can."

That brings him two steps closer to me. "Tell me how to make it up to you."

*Help me feel things I've never felt before.*

I keep that to myself as I tilt my head to the left. "I need to give that some thought."

"Would a kiss help?" His tongue drags a slow path over his bottom lip.

I'm mesmerized by it. Staring at him, I watch as he steps even closer.

He rakes both hands through his mane of hair. "We could try one kiss and see."

"One kiss," I repeat once he's standing in front of me.

His hand moves to my neck. Cupping it around the smooth skin, he fights off a smile. "Do you know how beautiful you are?"

The question sits on the edge of my tongue, so I ask it right back. "Do you know how beautiful *you* are?"

"You like the way I look?"

I raise my hand tentatively until it's resting on his jaw. I skim my thumb over his beard. "What's under this?"

"A man who wants to kiss you."

I push to my tiptoes and trace a finger over his bottom lip before I press my mouth to his.

# Chapter 18

## *Athena*

He kisses me as if I'm the only thing in the world that matters. I feel that. Right now, at this moment, I sense that I'm the only thing on his mind. I'm all he wants.

I melt into his embrace. His arms circle me. One hand glides down my back to the waistband of my jeans. I feel his fingers tap against me before his hand curls into a fist.

He's fighting it. He's fighting his desire to touch my skin.

I don't have that much self-control. I skim both of my hands over the front of his button-down shirt. My lips never leave his. Our kisses deepen with each second that passes.

My fingers start on a button on his shirt.

I want to see more of him. I'm craving the touch of his skin. Just as I undo the button, the jarring sound of a cell phone ringing draws him a step back.

I know it's not mine. I silenced it earlier. Work can wait until tomorrow.

Liam stares at my mouth as the phone rings inside the pocket of his pants. It stops but immediately starts again.

"Should you answer that?" I skim my fingers over my lips.

He shakes his head before he nods. "Dammit. Let me check who it is."

Pulling the phone out of his pocket, he holds it in front of him. "Rhys."

I'd ask who that is, but I can tell by his furrowed brow that it's someone who matters to him.

"You need to get that, don't you?"

"Athena." My name comes out like a plea between heaving breaths. "I'm sorry."

I rub a hand over my eyes, silently cursing his phone. "It's fine."

"Give me two minutes," he says before he turns to walk away.

The sound of a door shutting behind him sets me on a path to the sofa. I plop down on my ass, hoping that once Liam reappears, we'll pick up right where we left off.

***

It's been twenty-three minutes since Liam disappeared down the hallway.

I've responded to six Wild Lilac emails. I sent a text message to Jeremy asking when he can meet me for lunch so I can pick his brain about my advertising plans for the upcoming holiday season, and I saved a recipe for a southwest chicken salad to the notes on my phone.

I'll pick up everything I need to cook it and then go to Jeremy and Linny's house. Their kitchen looks like it belongs on the Food Network.

Mine consists of a hotplate, a small refrigerator, and a pair of mismatched plates with some utensils I found in a drawer when I moved in.

I love cooking, so for now, I'll take advantage of the open door policy at my brother and sister-in-law's brownstone.

I still feel at home there.

The sound of a soft knock on Liam's apartment door almost sends me off the edge of the sofa.

Startled, I twist around.

Whoever is on the other side, knocks again.

Smoothing a hand over my hair, I push to my feet, willing Liam to end his call and get out here.

Two more knocks fill the silence.

*Should I see who it is?*

I glance down the hallway, but the closed doesn't open. All I hear is the faint sound of Liam's voice.

Another knock from the apartment door draws me even closer to it. It could be a neighbor in distress, or maybe it's that ten-year-old girl Liam gave flowers to.

*It can't hurt to open it, right?*

I listen to my inner voice of reason and swing open the door.

"Hey, it's you." Darcy, the woman from the pirate -themed restaurant, shoots me a smile. "Athena, right?"

I step back when she pushes her way past me. "Can I help you?"

"You can't." She circles a finger in the air in front of my face. "Wolf can."

My gaze catches on a brown paper shopping bag in her hand.

"I'm here to drop off some of his things." With a bite of her bottom lip, she goes on. "He left them at my place. I thought tonight would be a perfect night to bring them over."

Walking away from the open apartment door, I fetch my purse and jacket before I head right back in the same direction. "He's on the phone."

She nods as if that's not news to her. "It figures. I'll make myself comfortable while I wait for him."

Running away isn't something I do, but I need fresh air. Whatever's in that bag in Darcy's hand is part of the relationship they once shared.

I don't need to hang around and watch the exchange of memories.

"I'll tell Wolf you had somewhere else to be." Her voice is laced with amusement. "It was good to see you again."

I can't say the same, so I exit the apartment and close the door behind me, leaving Liam and one of his ex-girlfriends behind.

# Chapter 19

## *Liam*

Did I step into a fucking time machine that's transported me eight months into the past?

Why is Darcy sitting on my sofa and not Athena?

I close my eyes, praying that when I reopen them, I'll see the woman I want to spend the night with in front of me.

I crack open one eyelid.

*Fuck. I'm still looking at Darcy.*

"Wolf!" She bounces to her feet. "There you are."

I ignore the fact that she's running her hands over the front of the tight red T-shirt she's wearing.

"Where's Athena?" I bark the question out as I look around the room.

Her purse isn't where she dumped it when she came out of the washroom before my call.

*Shit.* She's not here.

"Your friend left." Darcy jerks a thumb at the apartment door. "I needed time alone with you."

*For what?*

"How did you get into the building?" I brush past her on my way to the door. Swinging it open, I look to the left and the right, hoping that I'll catch Athena, but the corridor is empty.

"One of your neighbors held the lobby door for me." Darcy laughs. "He said he remembered that I'm a close friend of yours."

She's not. She's an ex that scared the living hell out of me when she started tailing me. I couldn't turn around without running straight into her.

Here at home.

At the gym.

My office.

You name it. If I was there, Darcy was close behind.

I ended it with the threat of a restraining order if she didn't keep her distance. My oldest brother, Sebastian, a sergeant with the NYPD, followed that up with a visit to her office encouraging her to move on. I didn't ask him to do it, but I thanked him for it.

I hadn't seen her again until she appeared at the seafood place the other night.

Slamming my apartment door shut, I head toward Darcy. "Get out."

That sets her back down on her ass on my sofa. She pivots so she's facing me, her long legs crossing as though she's settling in for the long haul.

I'm tempted to yank her up by the arm to toss her out, but I don't. I won't put a hand on her. In her twisted mind it would be akin to a marriage proposal. I intend to stay as far away from her as I can.

"You left a few things at my place." She points a long red fingernail at a brown paper shopping bag. "Check it out."

I know what's in there. It's the shampoo she bought for me that smelled like sour citrus. I hated it. It never touched my hair.

The clothes she picked out for me are undoubtedly in the bag too.

T-shirts with cartoon characters and a brand of jeans that I've never worn.

I turned it all down when she offered it and left it behind when I ended our short-lived relationship. She called me months ago to ask me what to do with it all. I told her to donate it or toss it in the trash.

"Take the bag and go home, Darcy." I cross my arms over my chest. "I told you never to come here again."

"When I saw you at the restaurant, I felt something between us."

"I can't speak for you, but from my end it was annoyance. Or frustration. Irritation maybe. Take your pick."

Her head tilts. "You don't mean that."

"I mean every word." I point at the door. "I'm leaving. You need to get out."

I'm about to chase Athena down. I left her alone for too long and then she had to deal with Darcy. I don't blame her for checking out of here without a word to me.

"Fine." She slides to her feet. "Sparky misses you."

"Your dog bit me, Darcy." I lead the way to the door. "I doubt like hell he misses me."

Trailing a finger over my back, she rounds me until she's standing right in front of me. "I bit you too. Do you remember?"

I can't say that I do.

The sex was sex. That's it. There was nothing attached to it but a need for release.

Swinging open the door, I ignore the question. "So long."

"So long?" she parrots back. "That's it?"

99

I wait until she's cleared the doorway before I respond. "That's it."

With a slam of the door in her face, I fish my phone out of my pocket and scroll to Athena's number.

I press dial as Darcy tosses out a few choice words that include what a fucking asshole I am.

She might be right. I don't care. I have one focus at the moment and that's Athena.

*Dammit. I wish she would answer the phone.*

# Chapter 20

### *Athena*

"How did you deal with all of Jeremy's…" my voice trails because what the hell? How do I ask my sister-in-law how she put up with all of my brother's ex-lovers?

I'm not an expert on what my brother did before he married his soul mate, but I could read between the lines.

He'd take off for a few hours at a time a couple of nights a week.

He was going to a hotel. I only know that because a key card fell out of the pocket of a pair of his jeans when I was doing the laundry.

I wanted to know why he needed a room at a hotel in Manhattan.

His stuttered explanation about visiting friends there was when the light bulb went on over my head.

Everything changed when he brought Linny home to meet us. I could tell he was in love the moment I saw the two of them together.

"All of Jeremy's what?" Linny asks as she adjusts a rose in a bouquet that I'm working on.

I should change the subject. Linny is at Wild Lilac to talk about advertising with me. She owns a boutique agency called Lincoln Dawn Communications. Her business is booming, but she still does pro bono work for me. I'm lucky to have her and Jeremy in my corner.

I swerve around her question because I have asker's remorse. "Do you think this bouquet has enough pink in it?"

It's all shades of pink.

"Cassidy would love it." A smile beams on her face when she mentions her little girl. She's our resident pink expert.

I was hoping that Linny would bring my niece with her to the shop, but Jeremy loves his Saturday mornings with his daughter.

It's sugar-coated cereal and cartoons for the two of them.

He only gives that up if his work takes him out of town.

"I'd say it's done." I pick up the vase with the roses and put it into the cooler.

"That Wild Lilac T-shirt is cute." Linny dusts her fingertips over my shoulder. "Your idea?"

"Al's," I admit. "He designed them for Leanna and me."

Settling onto a stool next to the table, Linny pushes her dark hair back from her forehead. "It's time to ditch the small talk. I could tell something was wrong when I called you last night. Spit it out."

Linny called me just as I was leaving Liam's building. I was in a hurry and I know she could hear the nervous quake in my voice.

We talked about work and Cassidy and by the time I was at the subway stop, my heart had slowed to a normal pace.

I said goodbye after I asked her to meet me here this morning.

Just as I was stepping onto the train, Liam called, but I didn't answer. He didn't leave a voicemail or send any text messages after that, so I went to bed.

Smoothing my palms over the front of my jeans, I let out a breath. "I met someone."

I've never uttered those words before. I've met plenty of men, but not one was worth talking about.

Linny's green eyes widen. "Someone? A man?"

"Liam," I offer his first name because I don't want him just to be *someone* or *that guy*. He's more than that to me already. I don't know if that's good or bad. I need Linny to help me figure that out.

Smiling, she claps her hands together. "Athena. I'm so excited for you."

I can tell she means it. Linny came into my life right when I needed her. I don't have any close friends. It's hard to form those bonds when you're fighting against the stigma that comes from having a mom and stepfather who stole from Manhattan's elite to line their own pockets.

"What's he like?" She leans her forearms on the table.

Memories of last night push everything aside. I could describe him as gorgeous and kind. Or sexy and an incredible kisser, but I don't. Instead, I trod down the petty route. "Popular."

"Popular?"

I opened the door, so I need to walk through it. "We haven't known each other long and I've already met two of his ex-girlfriends."

Before Linny can get her mouth open to say anything, I go on, "I met his most recent ex when I went to deliver flowers to her that he ordered. I met another ex when we were on a date. She showed up at his place last night with some of his things."

Her jaw tenses. "He sent flowers to one of his ex-girlfriends, and you delivered them?"

"She was his girlfriend at the time," I clarify, knowing that it makes zero difference in the big picture. "They broke up that night."

"I take it she didn't like the bouquet he chose?"

I know the question is meant to lighten the mood, but it's a reminder of the night we met. Liam would still be a stranger to me if it weren't for Wren.

"I think it went beyond that." I laugh.

"So that's ex number one." She wags her index finger in the air. "You said ex number two crashed your date last night?"

*In a very hard and unwelcome way.*

I don't know if Liam and I would have moved beyond kissing, but Darcy's sudden appearance took that decision out of my hands.

"When she knocked on the door, he was on a call in another room."

Linny's jaw tenses. "With who?"

I know what she's thinking, so I push that concern out of her mind with three simple words. "Not a woman."

Her shoulders relax. Tilting her head to the side, she stares at me. "What did you do when the ex showed up?"

I look away because I still don't know if I did the right thing. It felt right at the time. "I left."

"Good." She pushes to her feet. "You don't need to get tangled up with any guy who hasn't untangled himself from his past."

*What if I want to be tangled up with him?*

Moving closer to me, my sister-in-law sighs. "I can't tell you what to do, but I want your heart to be safe."

"Would you have dated Jeremy if you knew about all of his exes?"

Her eyes catch mine. "How many exes are we talking about?"

"Does it matter now?" I ask, reaching for the laptop. I slide it toward me so I can get started on my next order.

"No." She picks up a daisy I discarded earlier when I was going through my daily delivery. Bringing it to her nose, she closes her eyes briefly before she drops it back onto the table. "You matter. You're young. I know you haven't had the best luck with men, so be careful, Athena. Don't let this guy's baggage weigh you down."

Reaching behind me to pluck a single perfect pink rose from a container, I place it in her hand. "I promise I'll be careful. Give that to Cassidy for me and tell her Auntie Athena loves her."

"She loves you too." She plants a kiss on my cheek. "We all do. You'll come for spaghetti tomorrow night, right?"

"I wouldn't miss it for the world."

# Chapter 21

### *Athena*

Today was long as hell.

After Linny left, I dove into work and slammed out ten bouquets in record time.

*Boom.*

Only one of my weekend coworkers showed up. She brought with her an explanation for the other's absence. Martinis and men.

They both got drunk last night, so they flipped a coin and I ended up with a very queasy helper for the day. Since she was in no shape to face the people receiving the bouquets I put together, I took on deliveries again.

That's what brought me here.

I'm at the hospital.

It's almost eight p.m., so visitors are about to get the boot. I rushed to hand a pretty bouquet of irises to a new mom before a nurse shooed me away.

I shut down the shop before I left to come here, so my night is my own.

Scrolling through the food delivery app on my phone, I contemplate my choices.

I could stop and pick something up to save the delivery charge, or I could go super economical and eat whatever I find in my fridge that doesn't have a layer of mold on it.

My gaze bolts from a picture of a ham sandwich to my messaging app when I hear the chime signaling a new arrival.

I open the app.

**Liam: *Look up.***

My head darts up.

*What the hell?*

Standing across the lobby from me, dressed in dark jeans and a black Henley shirt is the man I haven't stopped thinking about since last night.

He closes the distance between us with heavy measured steps.

"Are you alright? Why are you here, Athena?"

I pull a deep breath in, trying to calm my pulse. Why do I feel lightheaded whenever I'm within a foot of him? "I'm fine. I was delivering flowers."

His face softens. "Good. That's good."

"Are you okay?" I question back because he's the last person I expected to see here on a Saturday night.

Scrubbing a hand over the back of his neck, he nods. "I'm fine too."

He doesn't add anything else, so I take it to mean that he's here because he's visiting someone. Maybe it's another ex. What is that saying about third times a charm? Or is it a nightmare?

"I want to talk." He inches closer. "Do you have time to do that now?"

I do, but I'm wiped out.

"There's a coffee shop a block from here." He jerks a thumb toward the lobby doors. "Are you in?"

I should be out. Linny's words of wisdom about Liam's past entanglements war with my desire, but this is an innocent cup of coffee. What's the harm in that? "I'm in."

When I start walking toward the doors, he falls in step beside me. Our fingers brush against each other, but I pull mine away. I need to keep my hands off of him until I'm sure that another one of his ex-girlfriends isn't going to pop up around the corner.

***

I take a seat across from him in a booth. We're in a coffee shop with worn red leather bench seats. Our table is propped up by a book under one uneven leg.

It's charming in an old-time New York City way.

The woman behind the counter knew Liam's name and his order by heart.

Everyone turned when she called out, "Wolf," to signal that our order of two medium coffees with cream and sugar was ready.

Blowing over the hot liquid in his cup, he keeps his eyes trained on my face.

*Am I supposed to start this conversation?*

"My brother is having a baby," he announces. "Sebastian. He's the oldest. Technically, his wife, Tilly, is having the baby."

I take a second to shift my thoughts from his ex-girlfriends to his brother. "Did you see her at the hospital?"

Nodding, he glances around the coffee shop. "She was there."

"Is she alright?"

I wouldn't know her if I passed her on the street, but I ask because he's tense. His hand is wrapped around the ceramic mug in a death grip.

"She's good." He half-smiles. "Happy. Excited to be a mom."

I take a sip of my coffee. It's bitter.

"Being an uncle is a pretty big deal." Leaning back, he exhales. "This will be my third time."

"I'm a one-time aunt." I push the mug away from me before I slide it closer again.

I didn't come here for small talk. I'm not even sure what I came for anymore. I yank my bag onto my lap. "I think I should go, Liam. I don't think this is going to…"

"Don't." His voice comes out strained. "I'm sorry about last night, Athena. I let you down."

He didn't. It's not his fault that Darcy showed up or that he had to take that call. That's all timing and circumstance. If anything, fate played a role in the night too.

"Darcy had no right coming over." He pinches the bridge of his nose. "We broke up months ago. I don't know what she was thinking showing up like that."

I know what she was thinking. *He's hot.*

She still wants him. I can't blame her for that.

"I was in the wrong place at the wrong time," I say before I swallow another sip of the bitter coffee.

"You were in the right place." He inches forward. "I really like you, Athena."

"I like you too," I admit.

Before I can tell him that I'm not a fan of coming face-to-face with his ex-girlfriends, he clears his throat. "I propose we lay our cards on the table right now."

I watch as he taps his hand on the tabletop.

"I have a past. I own it." His eyes lock on mine. "I can't erase any of it. I want you to know that I'm not interested in anyone but you. I know we said we're keeping it casual, and I'm good with that, but let me be clear that the only woman I want to hang out with is you."

Nervous, I spit the words out before thinking through what I should say. "My past isn't like your past."

*Did that sound as judgy as I think it did?*

For a second, I think I've offended him, but he cracks a smile. "Lucky you."

I can't leave well enough alone, so I try and explain. "I've only been with two men before. I've dated more guys, but I've only…"

Why did I tell him how many sexual partners I've had?

I need to keep my mouth shut.

He brushes his hair away from his forehead. "I wish my past was more like your past."

Sometimes I wish mine were more like his.

I don't regret not jumping into bed with more guys in college, but I wish that the men I had sex with were better partners.

More caring and loving, and it would have helped if they knew how to get me off.

"I've got a few ex-girlfriends in this city." He shakes his head. "But that's what they are. Exes. I don't want to reconnect with any of them."

"That's good to know."

He taps his palm on the table before he flips his hand over and motions for me to place my hand in his.

I do.

"Give me a chance to be your third, Athena."
He lowers his voice. "It doesn't have to be tonight or
tomorrow. Hell, I'm a patient man, but I want you. I
think I've made that clear."

*I want you too, Liam.*

The words play on my tongue, but they sit
there unspoken.

"Here's a plan." His eyes meet mine. "I'll
drop by your class on Tuesday, and if I show any
improvement in my floral design skills, you'll hang
out with me."

"After class?" I ask.

"After class," he affirms with a nod.

He comes with baggage, but I do too. Mine
isn't in the form of ex-boyfriends, but I still carry it
with me always.

I can't fault him for his past.

Glancing down at my hand nestled in his
palm, I nod. "It's a deal."

"I need to up my flower game." He laughs.
"Any pointers?"

I shake my head. "What fun is it if I help you
cheat? You're on your own, Liam."

"I'll figure it out." He leans back, still holding
tightly to my hand. "There's no way in hell that I'm
going to fuck up my chance for extra time with my
teacher."

# Chapter 22

### *Liam*

I made it within a block of my apartment before I turned around and headed back to the coffee shop.

I didn't forget anything. I'm not craving another cup of the bitter brew.

I left after kissing Athena on the forehead and watching her take off down the sidewalk headed home.

The temptation to follow her was strong, but if she wants me at her apartment at some point, she'll invite me.

I admit I'm surprised that she's only been with two men. She's beautiful and sensual in a way that is disarming.

My dick was throbbing as I sat on the uncomfortable red leather and watched her drink her coffee. I could have stayed in that spot for hours, but she was the one who called it a night.

"Wolf!" Rhys Quillan calls out to me as I round the corner headed for the café.

He sent me three text messages today. My phone sat in my pocket, silenced by order of the staff inside the hospital. I follow the rules if need be, and after a string of alerts, I was warned by a nurse to shut off my device.

I didn't go that far, but it was quiet enough that I missed Rhys's repeated attempts to reach out to me.

After I left the café earlier, he called, and I suggested we meet here. I know he lives within walking distance. I'm not billing him for this. He needs a few minutes of my time to get through the weekend. On Monday, he's back in class. His weekdays are filled with responsibility instead of the endless empty hours on Saturdays and Sundays that are devoted to memories.

He told me during our first session that the time between Friday afternoon and his first class of the week is his downfall.

Sporting newly bleached blond hair, Rhys raises an arm. "I'm over here."

He's impossible to miss. The sidewalk isn't as crowded as it was when I said goodbye to Athena. The city is winding down for the night.

Approaching him, I jerk a thumb at the door of the coffee shop. "This is the place. You didn't have trouble finding it?"

"I know this place." He glances at the paper menu taped to the window. "My mom used to bring me here for banana pudding after school when I was a kid."

He's only a decade younger than me, but I'd still label him as a kid. My jump from nineteen to twenty-nine was vast. I grew up once I graduated high school and hit college.

"We'll order you one of those," I half-joke.

His hands dart to cover his eyes.

*Shit. Fucking hell.*

I'm not an insensitive ass. I went into my line of work because of what I witnessed when I was a kid. My dad was always carrying the burden of the emotional pain he took on working as a detective with the NYPD.

My brother, Nick, lost his fianceé right around the time he was Rhys's age. I lived through that sorrow with him. I was overwhelmed by her death, but I helped pull him out of the darkness.

"Rhys," I start with a hand on his forearm. "Look, man, I'm…"

"She'd like it if I ordered it." He sucks in a deep breath. "She'd smile if she knew I was here."

*Hope.* It appears when you least expect it.

"I'll give it a try too," I say, tugging on the handle of the door to open it. "Grab a seat and I'll get two coffees and two banana puddings."

"Soda for me." He pats a hand on my shoulder. "My mom always told me the coffee here was bad as hell."

\*\*\*

"It's not half-bad, right?" I swing the bouquet I made in front of Athena.

Squeezing her eyes shut, she nods her head up and down. "It looks great, Liam."

*What the fuck?*

I huff out a laugh. "Open your eyes. Take a good look at it."

Squinting, she studies the mess of flowers in my hand. How the hell was I supposed to concentrate on her instructions? She's wearing a blue dress and for fuck's sake, her legs.

Her goddamn legs are perfection.

She's not tall, but they're perfect. Everything about her is everything I've ever wanted.

Leaning back, her gaze trails over my shirt to my face. "Do you want me to be honest?"

"Only if it means we're not saying goodnight in the next two minutes."

The corners of her lips quirk up. "I'd rate this as a solid six out of ten."

I'll fucking take it.

I shove the flowers into her hands. "I made it just for you."

She takes the bouquet. When she brings it to her nose, she inhales deeply. "Do you know that smelling flowers can put a person in a good mood?"

Being within ten feet of her puts me in a good mood. "Is that so?"

She offers the flowers to me, brushing them against the tip of my nose. "Try it."

I humor her by taking a whiff. "It works. I haven't been this happy in a long time."

Her eyes narrow. "You're serious?"

Her heels offer her extra height, but I still hover over her. I lean down until we're face-to-face. "I earned extra time with you tonight. That makes me a happy man."

She brushes the bouquet against my chin. "What's the plan?"

*Take you to bed. Taste you. Fuck you. Watch you come on my cock.*

If I want those things, I need to pace this right. "Let's start with a walk in the park."

"Central Park?"

I'd rather hop on the subway and head to my apartment with her by my side, but we'll get there if she's open to it.

I nod. "Put those flowers in water first. You don't want them to die."

"You're learning." She pats me in the center of my chest. "Another class and I think you may make it up to a seven."

"A man can dream." I laugh. "If my reward for improvement is more time with you, I'm prepared to do whatever it takes to work up to a perfect ten."

# Chapter 23

*Athena*

The fresh air did me good.

Walking through the city with Liam was calming. He did most of the talking. It centered on dozens of historical details about Manhattan. If he ever decides to give up his career as a counselor, he has a future in the past.

It was interesting and not just because I could listen to him talk about anything for days on end.

His voice is the sexiest I've ever heard.

I was enthralled when he told me stories about the architecture of certain buildings and the sordid past of their owners.

We walked for almost two hours before he flagged down a taxi. I didn't correct him when he told the driver to bring us to his apartment.

I could have asked him to drop me off at my place first, but I want more time with him.

"Water?" he asks as soon as he's locked his apartment door behind us.

"Please," I whisper back.

I'm parched. I'm also overheated. Late summer in the city is a mix. Last night it poured rain for hours. That left a bite of chill in the air. Tonight the humidity was off the charts.

I tug on the collar of the dress I'm wearing.

I only own a few, and since today was a special occasion, I decided to dress up.

I had a lunch date with Mrs. Ducat. She asked me to join her at the Waldorf. It happened once before, so I was quick to say yes. I brought a small bouquet of white roses for her, and she picked up the tab for the delicious meal.

We talked about flowers, her late husband, and her upcoming Caribbean cruise.

I could tell that she needed the company when she asked me yesterday if I liked the food at the Waldorf.

"Here you go." Liam shoves a glass of chilled water into my palm.

I swallow it down in three gulps. The entire time I keep my gaze trained to his face.

I watch him drink his water. His bicep bulges as he lifts the glass to his mouth. When he works on a swallow, his Adam's apple bobs up and down.

He's pure masculine rawness.

I move around him to set my empty glass on the edge of the coffee table.

Nerves jitter inside me, bouncing around. I push my hair back from my forehead, wishing that I had tied it up before class tonight.

"Are you as hot as me?"

That turns me back around to face him.

*Oh my God.*

He's yanked the hem of his T-shirt up to reveal perfectly sculpted abs.

"Would you mind if I took this off?" he growls with a glint in his eye. "No pressure for you to do the same, but I'm about to pass out."

I nod because every word I've ever learned is stuck in my throat.

He tugs on the back of the shirt. Before I know it, it's on the floor.

I knew he was gorgeous, but this is incredible.

His body looks like it belongs to a Greek God who has been carved in stone. His tattoos reach over his chest in a blend of grays and blacks. A thin line of hair trails from his belly button, disappearing beneath the waistband of his jeans.

He toes out of his boots and then drops his socks.

He rakes his hair until it's a messy blend of blond and brown around his face.

One hand drops to his stomach. "I still have that questionable candy bar in the drawer if you're hungry."

I shake my head. "I'm good."

"Good." He pops a brow. "Tell me what you want to do, Athena."

*Touch you.*

I fist my hands together at my sides because it wouldn't be fair for me to run my fingers all over his perfect body while I'm still fully dressed.

"We can watch Netflix. Or talk or kiss." The last word leaves his lips wrapped in a soft smile.

I step out of one of my shoes, and then the other. "We can do all three."

He moves closer to me, stopping when he's a foot away. "The television is in my bedroom."

I close the distance between us with quick, unsure steps. "I don't know if I'm ready for…"

"Netflix and talking?" He reaches out a hand. "Kissing if it feels right. No pressure."

In my mind's eye, I was the siren who would seduce this gorgeous man into a lust-filled night, but he's more than I bargained for, and it's not just about the extra-large condoms.

It's him.

The way he looks at me. The way he talks to me and the way he kisses me.

All of it.

I can't let my heart take the lead on this. He doesn't want anything serious. I'm too smart to fall for a guy who just got dumped.

He offers me his hand. "We'll stay on top of the covers. I'll build a pillow wall between us if you want."

Laughing, I search his face for something, anything that will tell me that he's all right with my hesitation.

I see it when he winks at me. "Come with me, lilac. I'll take care of you."

I believe him, so I slide my palm against his and let him lead me straight to his bedroom.

# Chapter 24

*Liam*

My bedroom isn't going to make it onto the pages of any home interior design magazines.

It has the essentials. A king-size bed because I need it. The bedding is white. I like simple lines and a minimalistic look, so the only other pieces of furniture are two mismatched bedside tables.

I keep everything in the closet. It's not large, but it's big enough to house what I need.

I watch Athena's expression as she takes in the room.

Sheer curtains cover the window. Light doesn't interfere with my sleep, so I never bothered to find something to block the sunrise.

"This is nice." She looks up at me.

I flick on the television that's hung on the wall across from my bed. I know it's not ideal, but sometimes I need the sounds emanating from it to lull me to sleep.

My mind races at night. The white noise coming from the TV is sometimes all I need to drift off.

Athena stays locked in place just inside the bedroom door.

I take the lead and drop my ass on the bed. "I'll get to work on that pillow wall."

That lures a smile to her mouth. "You don't have to do that."

I will if it gets her beside me.

She takes tentative steps toward the bed. Once her knees hit the mattress, she crawls on.

I watch her settle, with her back against the large wooden headboard. It was a gift from Sebastian when he sold his apartment. I grabbed it when he offered because it fits this room better than the slim design headboard I inherited with the apartment when I bought it.

Her hands skim over the skirt of the dress, adjusting it to cover her thighs.

I want to know what's under it.

I'm dying to see her skin, her tits, and her pussy.

I suck in a breath to try and will my cock to rein it in.

The scent of her skin is driving me mad. The second she's out the door tonight, my dick will be in my palm, pumping one out while I think about her underneath me.

"What do you want to watch?" Her voice envelops me. "What do you usually watch?"

"Whatever pops up first." I demonstrate by choosing the first thing in my '*recommended for you list*.' I drop the remote on the bedside table.

Her gaze leaves my face in favor of whatever the fuck is on the TV screen. I don't have that kind of self-control, so I stare at her profile.

I've met pretty women before, but she's different. The innocence in her face only adds to how alluring she is.

"You're not watching the show," she accuses without turning to me.

"You're way more interesting than whatever is on there."

That perks her brow. "You won't know that until you look at the TV."

Crossing my arms over my bare chest, I lean back against the headboard. My eyes never leave her. "I'm not going to look at the TV, lilac."

She swallows as her hands nervously knit together in her lap. "Can I touch you?"

My dick lurches inside my jeans. I close my eyes to ward off the desperation I feel.

"Yes." The word escapes me in a strangled whisper.

"I'll take off my dress first." She tugs on the material covering her thighs. "I want to leave everything else on for now."

I nod. "Whatever makes you comfortable."

Sliding her legs to the side, she moves to stand. I watch her undress with just the flickering light of the television illuminating her.

Her hand slides to a zipper at her side. She tugs it down slowly. Her breathing is audible. I can hear the excitement in it. I can sense she's nervous by the shaking of her hand.

With a tug down, the dress falls from her shoulders and pools at her feet to reveal a black bra and a pair of black boy shorts.

When she tips her head back, her hair bounces around her face.

It's the most beautiful thing I've ever seen in my life.

Without a word, she drops both hands on the bed and crawls back on. Her tits jiggle with each movement. Her hair swings back and forth.

Once she's beside me, I manage a question. I don't know how the fuck I string together the words, but they come out. "Should I take off my jeans?"

With a slide of her eyes over my chest and down to my lap, she nods. "Yes, please."

I unbutton the fly, shift on my ass, and push them down.

I don't try and hide the bulge in my black boxer briefs. Why the hell would I? I'm not ashamed of how much I want her.

"Can I touch you now?" she asks in a breathless voice.

I lean back again, setting my hands at my side because this is for her. This is all for her. "Be my guest, lilac."

# Chapter 25

### *Athena*

I kneel on the bed at his side. I glance over his body, taking in every single inch of exposed skin. I've never been with a man who looked like this before.

With just a fingertip, I touch his bicep.

The skin is soft, but the muscle underneath isn't.

He's hard as a rock.

I try not to stare as I run my finger up and over his shoulder, tracing a path over one of his tattoos.

When I reach the center of his chest, my gaze catches on his.

He's quiet. In silence, he watches as I circle a finger over one of his nipples before I move to the other.

"You must work out for hours every day," I whisper.

That draws a hearty laugh from him. His chest rumbles with it. "I hit the gym when I have the time."

I don't. My exercise routine consists of knee lunges at the flower shop and jogging in place while I wait for the subway.

I haven't looked at his lap since he took off his jeans, but I know what's there.

It's obvious that he's a big man in every way.

I know that from his confession about the size of his condoms, but I see it myself.

Resting back on my heels, I trail my fingers over his stomach. "Your body is perfect."

Patting a hand to the center of his chest, he shakes his head. "It's not. It's mine though, so I make the best with what I have."

Desire pools inside of me. What he has is exactly what I want.

I should slide my body over his and let him take me. I know he can make me feel things I haven't before. That's already happening, and we're not even fully undressed yet.

Tracing my hand over his chest, I move it to his chin. "Have you always had a beard?"

His hand lands on mine. "Do you like it?"

Nodding, I smile. "I do, but I wonder what you look like without it."

"Like a stranger," he admits on a sigh. "Like someone I don't recognize."

I feel that way sometimes when I look in the mirror. I don't know who my dad is. I imagine he looks like me since I look nothing like my mom. Sometimes my reflection reminds me that I'll never know everything I want to know about myself.

"Can I kiss you?" he asks with a tilt of his head. "I'll keep my hands to myself."

Taking a leap of faith is the only way I'll get to experience more with this man.

When I swing one leg over him, he growls out a sound that shoots straight to my core. His hands find my waist. Holding tightly, he adjusts me in his lap.

I settle on him, with his thick cock pressed against me, and my hands tangled in his hair.

"Kiss me," I whisper against his lips.

His lips part, his tongue darts over his bottom lip, and he tugs me closer until our mouths meet in a fierce, frenzied kiss.

\*\*\*

I rub myself against him. He's thick and wide. He may be shrouded in his boxer briefs, but there's no question that he's as aroused as I am.

Mewling, I lick my tongue over his bottom lip.

"Jesus, lilac." His voice escapes in a groan. "I want you."

I want him too. Desperately and madly. I want to come.

I grind myself into him, not caring that a barrier separates his cock from my pussy.

"Keep. Doing. That," he spits out each word harshly.

I throw my head back as my body heats from the inside out. I got myself off this morning in the shower when I thought about him, but it wasn't like this.

Nothing has been like this before.

He inches his hips up, carving small circles for me to ride on.

I take it all, shifting so my clit is resting against him. My hands slide down to his shoulders. I leverage myself as I chase an orgasm. My first orgasm with him.

"Fuck." His eyes widen. "You're going to come, aren't you? Say yes. Fucking say yes."

"Yes," I almost scream.

His hands tighten on my waist, helping to control my movement as I ride him shamelessly, not caring what I look like.

"Your tits," he breathes out in a twisted moan. "They're beautiful."

I look down to catch his gaze stuck on the front of my bra. "Undo it. Take it off."

He reaches behind me with one hand. In an instant, the clasp is free, and the bra is sliding down my arms.

He tosses it somewhere behind me.

"Oh, fuck." One of his hands leaves my side as he reaches for my breast. "So pretty. Such pretty pink nipples."

I throw my head back with a moan when I hear those words. When his mouth finds one of my nipples, I teeter on that edge.

It's that edge of release. It's the moment before my body splinters into a thousand shards of pleasure.

I rock back and forth, using his cock to chase my desire, and when I come, he bites my nipple hard, sending me straight into a second orgasm that steals my breath and leaves me trembling in his arms.

# Chapter 26

### *Liam*

By the time I walk back into my bedroom, Athena is fully dressed.

I expected as much. As soon as she came, she rolled off of me, curled into a ball on her side, and worked to catch her breath.

I cradled her from behind with my bare chest pressed against her back.

I wanted to slide those boy shorts down and fuck her, but she was spent.

When she asked me to get her a glass of water, I took off for the kitchen without question.

I knew that the odds were high that she'd be aching to leave when I got back.

"Thank you," she says when I hand her the water.

She drinks two sips before shoving it back in my hand. "I think I should go."

I've never dealt with this before. The moments after sex for me usually involve my head between my partner's legs until she comes again.

Athena isn't looking for more, and even though my dick has settled to the point that it's only semi-hard, I'm aching to touch her again.

"I'm sorry," she mutters under her breath. "I'm sorry, Liam."

I set the glass of water on the bedside table. "Hey, no. Don't say that."

Her eyes dart over my face in a panic. "It was a lot for me. That was the best…I've never done that before with a man."

I don't want to be insensitive, but I need to ask. "What do you mean?"

"I don't come with men," she admits with her gaze on the floor. "Only by myself."

*What the ever-loving fuck?*

Is she serious?

Who the hell has she been sleeping with?

I don't press because that pink hue on her cheeks tells me that it wasn't an easy confession for her to make.

"I can take you home," I offer as I round the bed looking for my jeans.

"No." Her head shakes. "I can get there on my own."

She needs space. I'll give it to her. I'd be an asshole not to.

I slide my jeans up before I turn back to face her.

*Christ.* I don't want this to be awkward. I want this to be our beginning. I don't give a shit that I didn't get a release out of this. I got something better. I watched her splinter. I saw the way her lips parted. I felt her come on me.

That's better than any fuck I've ever had.

I have no idea where her mind is, so I ask a question I need an answer to. "I'll see you again, right?"

If she says no, I'll drop to my knees and beg. I'll crawl after her if I have to.

"Yes." She answers with a subtle dip of her chin. "Maybe this week?"

"Tomorrow," I spit out before I consider what I've got going on.

"I can't." She shrugs. "I have an appointment with Audrey tomorrow night to go over the order for her wedding flowers."

I should tag along on that, but I don't need Audrey to know that Athena and I are seeing each other. She's a friend of Wren's. I don't want the complication.

I have appointments that run late on Thursday, so I opt for the first available day. "Friday?"

"I can do Friday," she affirms with a smile.

"I'll cook something," I say without thinking.

I doubt she's going to be impressed with scrambled eggs and bacon or a toasted bagel.

Adjusting the waist of her dress, she glances at me. "I'd like that, Liam. Should I bring anything?"

"Just you," I answer quickly. "I'll see you on Friday at seven, Athena."

A faint smile crosses her lips as she heads out of my bedroom.

I glance back at the bed. Tonight I only got a taste. On Friday, I hope I get more.

\*\*\*

Four appointments filled my afternoon, but I'm only rounding the homestretch. The finish line is still hours away.

My Wednesday has been spent counseling folks who found their way to me after they lost someone that mattered to them.

I've never known two people who journey through grief the same way. Some can't put one foot in front of the other, while others plaster on a brave face and barrel through their lives, ignoring the pain that is strapped to their backs.

I do what I can for every single person who sits across from me.

When I started this job I was confident that I could make a difference in the world. My impact may not be as wide-reaching as I thought it would be, but I'm doing what I can to guide people toward a future where the pain finds a place it can settle without overwhelming everything else.

I approach my office door when I hear Audrey calling my name.

When I round the corner into the corridor, she's on the approach with her hands waving in the air.

"Tell me that you're free on the last Saturday of next month."

"You tell me if I am." I cross my arms over my chest. "Winola gives you the schedule to send out."

We're only open two Saturdays a month, and I usually land one half-day shift. Winola likes to work weekends since some of her high profile clients slip in to see her.

She's owned this office for close to thirty years.

When she offered me the chance to work alongside her to get my bearings after I graduated from college, I jumped on the opportunity.

I moved into an empty office when one of the other counselors relocated to Boston.

I've been here ever since.

"You're free." Audrey swings her arms at her sides. "Everyone is free. We're closed that day in honor of my wedding."

*Fuck.* I know what's sitting on the tip of her tongue.

"You'll come if I invite you, won't you?" Her eyelashes flutter. "I want the whole gang there."

The people who work at Dehaven Center have never been a *gang*.

Seeing Wren is not at the top of my list of things to do, and I know she'll be there. I'm not one for coming up with excuses on the fly, so I buy myself some time. "I'm going to run to get a coffee before my next appointment. Do you want one?"

"Two sugars and a splash of cream." She sets off toward her desk. "Oh, and before I forget, I'm leaving a few minutes early today. I have an appointment with a florist for the wedding. Wild Lilly is the name the shop."

"Lilac," I correct as I breeze past her desk on my way to the elevator. "It's Wild Lilac, Audrey."

Pushing open the double glass doors, I stroll through before I jab a finger into the elevator call button.

"My lilac," I let the words slip off my tongue in a whispered tone. "She's my wild lilac."

# Chapter 27

*Athena*

Opening the small heart-shaped gold locket in my hands, I squint at the faded pictures of an older man and woman. I've been doing the same thing every week or two since I was ten-years-old.

I should be ashamed of myself.

The locket doesn't belong to me. It belongs to a man my mom had a one-night stand with twenty-four years ago.

He took her home after they met at a bar. When she woke, he was still asleep, so she filled her pockets with whatever she could fit in them and took off.

Nine months later, I was born.

She never told the man she slept with that he had a daughter. She didn't tell the other two men she had one-night stands with that she was carrying their sons.

My two younger brothers have no idea who their fathers are either.

Every few years after we were all born, my mom would get married in an attempt to give us a father figure.

It wasn't until her third marriage that everything changed. She married Jeremy's dad, and we finally had a family, including an older brother.

Now, my mom and my stepfather, Craig Weston, are in prison.

I still have a family, but there are questions too. Questions about the man my mom took this locket from.

Ending her call, Audrey finally turns back to me with a bright smile. "That took forever, didn't it?"

*Fourteen minutes, but it felt like forever.*

Audrey's been at Wild Lilac for more than an hour waiting on her matron-of-honor to show up, but from what I just overheard, the woman is miles away from Manhattan.

"It looks like I'm going to do this on my own." Slapping her hands together, she braces her designer heels a few inches apart as if she's readying for a battle. "I think I know exactly what I want."

If she does, I'll be surprised.

She spent the first twenty minutes here trying to find a rose that matches her suit jacket. It's an odd mix of pink and orange.

When I was able to get her back on track, she waffled between an all-white theme for the ceremony flowers or a brightly colored mishmash of whatever caught her eye in the store.

"Do you think I'm elegant?" She spins in a circle.

I don't want to offend her, so I smile and nod. "Very."

"I think all white with splashes of pink is the way to go." She pats the arm of her jacket. "Can you show me some samples?"

I move toward my laptop. "I have an online gallery. I can show you the photos of a wedding I did three months ago. I think that might be what you have in mind."

Her phone chimes behind me. "Oh, it's Wren!"

I lose a half a step on my way, but I keep my shoulders back and avoid falling into the trap of thinking about Liam's ex-girlfriend.

Tapping my fingers on my laptop keyboard, I catch Audrey doing the same on her phone.

"I'm going to sit her right beside Wolf at the wedding," she announces in a giddy tone. "I still think they belong together."

*He belongs with me.*

I chant that silently to myself over and over again wishing it were true, even though I know that he's only looking for something fleeting and fun.

*** 

After a busy morning designing and creating four large arrangements for a new office opening on Park Avenue, I sneak out of the shop to grab something to eat. Leanna can handle things until I get back. I need fresh air, food, and time to myself.

Ever since Audrey mentioned Wren to me last night, I've been thinking about what's going to happen when Liam sits down next to her at the wedding.

I don't know if old sparks will reignite.

Maybe he'll find another seat at a table across the room from her.

The wedding isn't for another few weeks, so I might not even be a part of his life at that point.

I want to be.

Weaving through the midday pedestrian traffic, I spot the broad shoulders and messy hair of the man I can't get out of my mind.

Liam is headed right toward me.

I raise a hand to try and grab his attention, but his eyes are buried in his phone.

*He's brave.*

I keep my eyes on the people around me whenever I set out down the sidewalk in this city.

Trusting people to look out for you is hard when those you trust most in the world let you down.

"Athena." My name leaves his lips the moment he looks up and spots me.

I skip around two people walking hand-in-hand, and a woman who has her fingers wound tight around the leash of a very friendly dog.

I pat it on the head before I stalk toward Liam.

"I was coming to see you," he says as he pockets his phone. "I have something for you."

My gaze drops to a white paper bag in his hand. "What is it?"

"Toasted sourdough bread, cream cheese, and a container of mixed berries. I threw in a candy bar just like the one you had in your bag, and a bottle of water."

*Wow.*

No one, other than Linny or Jeremy, has gone to this much trouble for me. I try to find the right words. "I'm grateful…thank you…you're kind."

"I'm selfish." He shoves the bag into my hand.

Looking down, I ask the obvious question. "Selfish? Why would you say that?"

"I was hoping that bringing you lunch might end with a kiss for me."

I look up into his beautiful eyes. Memories of what we did two nights ago flash in front of me.

Rising to my tiptoes, I rest a hand on his shoulder and smile. "It deserves more than a kiss."

"I'll collect on Friday night," he says before he presses his lips to mine in a lingering, soft, delicious kiss.

When he pulls back, my knees wobble. I step forward, my boot landing on the toe of his. "That was nice."

With a brush of a finger over my cheek, he drops his voice to a low tone. "I'm going to count every fucking hour until I see you on Friday, lilac."

"Me too," I admit on a sigh.

"I have to get back to work." He looks up at the sky. "Damn this earning a living thing."

I let out a laugh. "Thank you again for lunch, Liam."

"My pleasure." He tilts his head. "I'm going to sear the memory of what you look like right now into my mind until I see you again."

I look like I've been working my ass off. I'm wearing a wrinkled Wild Lilac T-shirt and ripped black jeans.

With a glance down at his watch, he lets out a muted curse. "I need to run. Promise me you'll eat every last bite."

"Every last bite," I repeat back before he glides his lips over my forehead and takes off at a slow jog down the sidewalk.

# Chapter 28

## *Liam*

I don't know what the hell I'd do without my family. I glance at the framed picture hanging on the wall of all of us that a waiter took at a restaurant in Greenwich Village a few months ago.

We were gathered there to celebrate Sebastian's birthday.

It was a good night. I went solo because I've never felt the pull to introduce a woman I'm seeing to my family.

The itch is there now.

I know my brothers would love Athena. Nikita would want to talk shop with her since they both run businesses.

My parents would welcome Athena with open arms.

"That's my favorite picture." My mom taps me on the shoulder. "When you get married, we'll take a new one."

I spin around to face her. "When I get married? What about Nikita?"

"Candy is that girl's life." My mom swats a palm over the front of the navy NYPD T-shirt I'm wearing. "How can she meet a man if she spends all her of time handing out treats?"

"She owns a very successful candy store," I point out. "She built that place from the ground up by herself. Maybe all she wants right now is to focus on that."

I'll be my sister's cheerleader any day of the week because I know she'll step up to bat for me if need be.

She's talked my parents down from the marriage ledge before. They want to see all four of their children happy, but they forget that not all life stories have to end with a wedding and kids.

"Put the chicken in the oven for an hour, give or take." She wipes her hands on the apron that's tied around her waist. "Toss the potatoes onto the pan thirty minutes before you eat and the asparagus twenty-five minutes after that."

"Got it," I say with a brisk nod.

"I wrote it down for you." She jerks a thumb over her shoulder toward the kitchen. "I brought a chocolate cake for dessert. It's Keats's favorite."

*Good for him.*

When I mentioned to my mom via text yesterday that I was going to cook dinner for a friend, she assumed it was Keats since he's the only person who ever shows up here for a meal.

Typically, he brings take-out, but my mom popped by unannounced one night when Keats was practicing his spaghetti making skills.

My mom took over and prepared a feast for both of us.

I didn't ask her to make the trek down here today with groceries in hand, but I sure as hell didn't order her out of my kitchen.

She tugs on the short hairs of my beard. "You look tired, Wolf."

Cradling her hand in mine, I kiss her open palm. "I'm fine."

Pushing her glasses up the bridge of her nose, she looks me over from head-to-toe. "You should go to bed after dinner."

*That's the plan.*

"I need to go," she announces. "Your dad and I are meeting friends for dinner at a new bistro."

Pushing her fingers through the brown curls on her hair, she glances up at me. "How do I look?"

"Beautiful," I say without hesitation. "You're the best. Never forget that, mom."

Patting me on the cheek, she smiles. "I promise I won't. Save the leftovers and soak the pan before you put it in the dishwasher."

Memories of my childhood in the cramped apartment we lived in uptown flood over me. I pulled dishes duty almost every week. It meant one-on-one time with her, so I never complained.

"Do you want me to walk you to the subway stop?"

"Nicholas taught me all about Uber," she says as she heads for her leather bag slung over the back of one of the chairs in the living room. "It's my new thing."

I smile at the grin on her face. "Looks like you're set."

"I love you, son." She steps toward me, pointing a finger at the framed picture. "We all do."

I know they do. I'm a lucky man. I've got my family behind me, and an evening in front of me with the most beautiful woman in Manhattan.

\*\*\*

"I come bearing gifts." Athena pushes a small round vase filled with purple flowers into my hands. "I hope you don't mind."

Why the fuck would I mind?

She showed up to my apartment dressed in a purple silk blouse, black jeans, and a touch of pink lipstick on her mouth.

I set the flowers in the middle of my coffee table. "Please work your magic."

Tossing her purse at me, she walks over to the table and spins the vase half a turn. "It's perfect, isn't it?"

My eyes are glued to her ass. "So perfect."

She taps the tip of her nose with her index finger. "Something smells delicious. Are you a good cook?"

Why the hell would I lie to her?

I own up when I place her purse on the arm of a chair. "My mom came by and got everything started."

That sets her gaze over my shoulder and toward the kitchen. "Is she here? You didn't say anything about her being here. I would have brought her flowers too."

*Of course, she would have.*

I rub a finger over my bottom lip. "She took off twenty minutes ago."

Relief draws her shoulders forward. "It was nice of her to cook dinner for us."

I make a mental note that Athena is parent shy. If this stays on track, I'll ease her into meeting the Wolf family at some point. I'll start with one of my brothers or maybe a sister-in-law first.

I shake off the vision of her eating dinner here with my brothers and their families.

"It's ready if you are." I point at the kitchen.

I'm not a hurried host, but I want dinner over so I can feast on her body.

"I'm famished." She rubs a hand over her stomach, pulling the material of her blouse taut over her tits.

I unpin my gaze from her and grab her hand. "Come with me, lilac. I think you're going to enjoy every bite."

# Chapter 29

*Athena*

Savoring the taste, I close my eyes.

I didn't just moan, did I?

Popping open an eyelid, I find Liam looking at me, his fingers stroking his beard. "I could watch you eat cake all night."

A smile teases my lips, but I fight it off. "You haven't touched your piece yet."

"I'm not in the mood for cake." He pushes the plate holding a large slice of the decadent treat to the side. "Take your time eating dessert. I'm enjoying the show."

I drop the fork onto the plate. "I can't eat if you're staring at me."

"I can't not stare at you," he counters.

I pick up the white linen napkin we've shared throughout dinner. He searched every drawer in his kitchen for its twin, but I told him I only needed a corner of it, so we agreed to make do with just one.

Our hands met on it a few times. He was always the gentleman, offering it to me first.

"I had enough." I eye the half-eaten piece of cake. "For now."

"For now?" He pushes his index finger into the icing before he drags it over the tip of his tongue. "Maybe later we can share a piece."

*Later. After we get into his bed.*

I knew what this night would entail. I didn't come to Liam's apartment thinking that we'd eat dinner and hang out.

The unspoken part of the invitation was that we'd have sex.

He wants to fuck me.

I don't just see it in the way he's looking at me. I felt it in his touch every time our fingers brushed against each other on the napkin.

"What's running through that mind?" He leans back in his chair. "Does it involve flowers?"

Until I met him, it did.

My store was my life. I spent every spare moment I had there and poured all of myself into its success.

Stepping away, even if it was just to have dinner with a man, felt wrong.

It doesn't feel that way with him. Being here is right. Tonight feels perfect.

I need a few more minutes to steady myself before we go to his bedroom, so I lean back in my chair too, crossing my legs at the knee. "Dinner was delicious."

"I'll tell my mom you said so."

His mom. I know that she has to be the woman with the brown curls in the picture hanging on the wall behind him.

She's in the center of a large group of people. Liam is standing to her left. Two men with jet black hair are on either side of her, and an older man with the same dark shade of hair, but peppered with gray is hugging her from behind.

There are three women in the picture too. They're almost as beautiful as the two little girls.

That's Liam's family.

I dart my eyes from the silver frame when I realize I was staring.

"Does your mom ever cook for you, Athena?"

My hand jumps to my neck and the gold locket. Nestled inside are the two pictures of strangers who may or may not be related to me.

I've always taken comfort in the idea that they are.

"She was never a good cook." I sidestep his question. "My brothers and I picked up pointers from watching chefs on TV."

"So you're self-taught?" He narrows his gaze. "I bet you're a great cook."

"I haven't had many complaints."

That statement is true if you don't count my younger brothers, Zach and Breccan. They thought it was funny to pick apart every aspect of the meals I'd create for them. Deep down, I knew that they appreciated the effort. The three of us weathered a lot of storms together, and when we joined Jeremy's family, he helped us stay on course through bad times.

"Will you teach me how to cook?"

I can't tell if he's teasing or not, so I push for more. "You want me to teach you how to cook?"

"I'm a great student." He brushes a hand over the shoulder of his T-shirt. "You've seen me in action with a bunch of flowers and a vase."

I scrunch my nose. "I hope you're better with a spatula than you are with a daisy."

His face takes on a pained look. With a dart of his hand to the middle of his chest, he lets out a groan. "That hurt. I thought I was working my way closer to a ten."

146

"What's the reward if you make it all the way up to a ten?"

His eyes meet mine. "You naked in my bed for the night."

I thought that was the plan for tonight, but maybe it's not in his mind. Disappointment washes over me.

"Unless I've already earned a ten in setting the table." He reaches forward to tuck a strand of hair behind my ear. "It's your call, Athena."

I imagined he'd sweep me off my feet and take me to his bedroom, but if I have to make the decision, I will. "I give your table setting skills a solid ten."

His finger traces a path over my cheek. "You're sure?"

I think I am.

Before I can nod, he goes on, "I'll take things slow. If it gets to be too much, you'll tell me. Alright?"

He's sensitive to my needs and fears in a way I've never experienced with a man before. The other two men I slept with couldn't get me into bed fast enough. It was the same pattern when we fucked. Their release mattered to them more than anything I was feeling or what I wanted.

I lock eyes with him. "You're the most understanding man I've ever met."

His hand trails down my face until it cups the back of my neck. "I want you, lilac, but more than that, I want this to be good for you. I want it to feel right."

Nothing in my life has felt this right before.

Leaning forward, he presses a soft kiss to my mouth. "I'm going to clear the dishes. Why don't you head to the bedroom?"

He's giving me a minute alone to gather myself.

I need it.

"I'll be waiting for you," I whisper before I kiss him. "Don't be long."

# Chapter 30

*Athena*

I took off my clothes but couldn't bring myself to drop my bra or panties. It's not because I'm ashamed of my body. I bought new lingerie months ago but decided to save it for a special occasion.

When I dug the white lace bra and panties out of my dresser drawer this morning, I smiled. I hadn't remembered that the bra had pink stitching or that it was so soft.

I put it on and twirled in a circle in front of my bathroom mirror. I liked how I looked from every angle. I know Liam will like it too.

I settle in on top of the covers. My back is pressed against the headboard. My legs are crossed at the ankles, and my stomach is doing double flips inside of me.

I want this. There's no question about that.

Nervous energy is coursing through me in anticipation. The last time I was in bed with Liam, I came apart from sheer pleasure. I don't know what's going to happen once he's inside me.

I feel like this is my first time all over again.

"Hey."

I look up to find Liam at the doorway to his bedroom. The light from the hallway is illuminating him from behind.

He's tall and broad and without any doubt, he's the sexiest man I've ever seen in my life.

He tugs the T-shirt he's wearing over his head as he steps closer to me.

With his gaze pinned to me, he drops his jeans. I wait for the boxer briefs to follow, but he keeps them on.

Standing next to the bed, he rakes me over. His voice comes out low and filled with need. "You're so fucking beautiful."

I feel it. He makes me feel it.

The mattress dips when he drops a knee to it. I'm tempted to scoot over to give him room, but I don't. I stay in place, anticipation ripping a path through me.

I'm already wet and needy.

His hand moves slowly over the blanket until it slides onto my knee. I shiver under the touch. His hand is warm. There's comfort in the way he circles his index finger over my skin.

I close my eyes when his hand glides up my thigh.

"I need to make you come," he rasps. "I haven't stopped thinking about the last time you were here. Those sounds you made. The way you looked. Jesus, it was everything, lilac."

Without another word, he slides off the bed and drops to his knees. His hands circle my calves. "Move here. I need you closer."

I shuffle on the bed, trying not to let out a moan. I know what's coming. I know I'll be coming.

He takes over my movements, sliding me to the edge of the bed. With his hands on my thighs, he parts my legs.

When he drops his head and licks a long path over my panties, I shudder.

A scream catches in my throat the moment he tugs the lace aside, and his tongue glides along my cleft.

"You taste so good," he growls. "So damn good."

His words fall victim to the pounding desire inside of me. With my hands wrapped in the strands of his hair, I push myself against his mouth and ride his tongue to a climax that feels like it breaks me in two.

\*\*\*

A word doesn't exist to describe what I'm feeling right now.

Liam licked me until I settled after I came. With soft kisses on my inner thighs, he pulled my panties down my legs.

His breath tickled my already swollen wetness, and when I thought he was about to push back to stand, he speared his tongue into me.

I yelped before a moan escaped me in a sound that was so twisted with need that he told me he was about to come.

He's on his feet now, his boxer briefs on the floor, and his beautiful cock in his hand.

He's sheathing it with a condom he yanked out of the nightstand drawer.

I can't take my eyes off of him.

It's not just his impressive body. It's him.

He's gentle in a way I never knew existed, but there's more there. I felt it when he slid a finger into me just as I came a second time. His touch was demanding.

He fucked me slowly with his finger, sliding in a second and then another to ready me for what's to come.

"Don't judge me based on tonight." He huffs out a laugh. "I'm not a minute man, but I swear to fuck that I'm not going to last."

Crawling onto the bed, a smile takes over his mouth. "You're gorgeous. If I drop dead tonight, I will have lived a happier life than most men."

I throw my head back in laughter. "You're not going to die, Liam. I might. Look at that thing."

Cupping his cock in his palm, he raises a brow. "This thing?"

Reaching behind me, I unhook my bra. "You'll go slowly, won't you?"

"She asks me that right before she flashes the most beautiful set of tits in the world."

I settle back on the bed. "You've made tonight special for me."

He crawls over me until his hands bracket either side of my head. "It's just as special for me."

I give in to it then, to the overwhelming need to be with this man.

His lips find mine as he notches the tip of his cock against my opening. When he pushes in, pain bursts through me, but I breathe. I take slow breaths as he slides in and then out, each time a little deeper.

His thrusts are smooth and measured as I adjust. His lips never leave mine. Our uttered sounds and unspoken words mix together as we find our rhythm.

"I need more," he says through clenched teeth. "I need more."

I twist my hands in his hair. "Give me more."

He does. He fucks me hard with a hand on my hip and my name falling from his lips.

Writhing beneath him, I claw at his shoulders, unrecognizable words pour out from my between my lips. I race over the edge and into an orgasm that blurs everything but him.

With a roll of his fingers over my clit, he chases his release, and when he comes he roars my name.

# Chapter 31

### *Liam*

I begged her to spend the night with me, but Athena left after we fucked.

I didn't let her run right out the way she did last time. I cradled her in my arms and told her a story about the history of Grand Central Terminal.

She asked questions and laughed when I knew every answer.

This city has always fascinated me. When I was a kid, I'd spend my summers researching the little known facts about centuries-old buildings and the people who once lived and worked there.

I can't say the building I work in is seeping with history, but there have been a lot of stories shared there.

I'm standing on the sidewalk in front of it waiting for Rhys.

It's Saturday afternoon, and I'm not pulling a shift today, but he sent me a text message an hour ago saying he needed an ear to listen.

I was here going through some of my files, so I told him to meet me outside.

Winola is upstairs in a session with a senator who lost his son recently. Discretion is all he wants, so I slipped out of the office unnoticed. Meeting Rhys there won't work today.

"Hey, Wolf!"

I turn to the left to see him approaching. His blond hair is gone. It's been replaced with a dark shade of green.

He's pulling it off.

"Rhys." I point at finger at his head. "You're a brave man. I like the new look."

"Before my mom lost all of her hair, she dyed it a different color every week." He scrubs a hand over the back of his neck. "She wanted me to join her, but I didn't. I regret that now, you know?"

I know.

Regret can crowd the heart after death, leaving little room for anything else.

Rhys seems to have a handle on it though. He's celebrating his mom by honoring her. He's not wallowing in the *what-might-have-been* pit.

"She'd be proud of you for taking on the task now."

I mean every word of it. Deidre was proud of her son. It shone through in every word she spoke about him. The kid was the light she needed to push through the pain of her treatments. She fought to the end for him.

"Do you want to get a hotdog or something?" He pats the back pocket of his jeans. "My treat."

If he needs someone to hang out with for an hour or two, I've got the time. "I'm hungry. Let's go."

We start down the sidewalk, side-by-side. When we reach the corner, he turns to face me. "My dad's warming up to the idea of coming to see you."

That's good news. Deidre worried about her husband Gareth. She hoped that one day he'd be ready to open up and talk about her death. That day may be closer than I anticipated.

"I told him about the idea of shooting hoops." Rhys mimes tossing a basketball. "He liked that."

I'll do whatever it takes to get him to open up. I made a promise to his wife that I'd help him and their son. I fully intend to follow through.

"Does he know what I'm working with?" I flex my right bicep. "Is he sure he wants to take this on?"

"I told you that my dad has some moves on the court, Wolf." He steps onto the street once the light changes. "He may surprise you."

I fall in step beside him again. "We'll see."

"You could hold back and let him win." He smiles. "My mom would do that when they played cards."

I can see that. Deidre was the type of woman who would give you the shirt off her back and help you put it on.

"I can't make any promises, Rhys." I toss him a wink. "You get him to the court, and I'll size him up."

"Deal." He jerks a thumb to the left. "That hot dog cart is the best in the city. My folks took me there for the first time when I was five."

Memories like that are what will get him moving forward. It's my job to make sure he keeps heading in that direction.

\*\*\*

An hour later, I stand and gaze into the windows at the front of Wild Lilac. Athena is inside talking to two women.

She's smiling in that way that melts every heart within a thousand miles. I've seen it when we've been out for dinner or during her classes.

She puts everyone at ease. Her voice is soothing and calm. It's impossible not to fall in love with her, and I swear to God, that's what is happening to me.

I should go in and sweep her off her feet.

I doubt like hell that anyone inside the store would mind if I gathered her in my arms and kissed her senseless.

I want to.

She made my night last night. She's made my year. Hell, she's making me imagine a life where I can be happy every day. A life where the past doesn't matter and the future is brighter than I ever imagined it could be.

My phone's alarm sounds in the pocket of my jeans.

I don't need to check it.

I fucking know what it is.

I tear myself away from the beautiful vision in front of me and take off down the sidewalk.

# Chapter 32

## *Athena*

I skipped through my weekend with a smile on my face. No one knew what that was about. When I went to Jeremy and Linny's brownstone for dinner last night, they both shot me looks. Neither of them asked why I was happy. They assumed it was because business has picked up at the store.

It has.

I arrived to work early on this Monday morning because I had a flood of online orders come in yesterday. Leanna is on her way in so we can tackle them together before Al shows up to handle the deliveries.

My life is falling into place in a way I never dreamed it could.

My business is picking up, and I'm seeing an incredible man.

I slept with that man on Friday, and my body is still thrumming from that experience.

*Who the hell knew that sex could be that good?*

I look up when I hear the bell ring over the shop door. Expecting Leanna, I wave a hand when I see my older brother walking toward me.

"Jeremy?" I push to stand. "What are you doing here?"

Holding out his arms, he motions for me to embrace him. I do.

I've always found comfort in my oldest brother's arms. He was the anchor that held me steady when my mom and his dad were sent to prison for stealing from the clients of the investment firm they ran together.

Jeremy took my brothers and me in and made sure we knew that his home was our home.

We fought through our mutual pain to build a strong sibling bond even though we're not related by blood.

I take a step back after we hug. "You didn't answer my question. Why are you here?"

He looks around. "I'm here to buy my wife flowers."

I know him better than that. When he wants flowers for Linny, he texts me and then insists I meet him somewhere for lunch with the bouquet in hand. Ever since I moved out, he's been worried that I don't eat enough.

I play along because when he's ready to tell me why he's really here, he will.

"What do you have in mind, Mr. Weston?" I tap a finger to my forehead. "If memory serves me correctly, your wife likes roses."

"My wife likes a lot of things." He crosses his arms over his chest. "You'd be interested to know what went on in our bedroom last night."

"Stop." I scrunch my nose. "I don't want to know about that. I'm your sister. We don't talk about stuff like that."

"Linny couldn't stop talking about you before she fell asleep." He reaches forward to inch my pink sweater up my arm to my shoulder. "She told me about Liam."

"What's there to tell?" I quip.

The only conversation Linny and I have had about Liam was focused on his ex-girlfriends. I thought she forgot all about him.

"She told me he has some baggage." He narrows his brown eyes. "Are you still seeing him?"

"Why are you asking me that?" I go for the confrontational approach because it's served me well in the past.

He rolls his eyes. "Linny sent me down here to find out why you were so over-the-moon happy yesterday."

Shrugging a shoulder, I chuckle. "It's a crime to be happy?"

"If it is you better lock me up and toss the key in the Hudson River because I am one happy son-of-a-bitch."

I love knowing that Jeremy has found the happiness he deserves. He's done so much for my brothers and I. He deserves to spend the rest of his life with the woman he loves raising their daughter.

"I don't care about how much baggage anyone carries on their back." He pats the shoulder of his gray suit jacket. "I care about the heart beating in your chest. I don't want this Liam guy to damage that. If he does, I'm going to hunt him down."

"We're having fun," I admit. "I like him, Jeremy. He's good to me."

"What about the reappearing exes?"

"They've disappeared into the ether." I wave a hand over my head. "They are officially out of sight and out of mind."

"Keep them that way," he says with a glance at the watch on his wrist. "Put together something for Linny and something pink for Cass. I'll meet you at Crispy Biscuit at noon."

It's one of my favorite diners. Jeremy loves the food there too.

"I'll be there."

Leaning forward, he plants a soft kiss on the tip of my nose. "I'm still getting used to this independent, grown-up version of you, so look the other way if I overstep a boundary or two along the way."

"You haven't overstepped." I pat his chest. "But I'm good at taking care of myself. I'm careful. I'll always be careful."

"That's all a big brother can ask for." He smiles. "I'm off to convince the world that Rizon Vodka is always the best choice."

"Good luck," I quip as he heads for the door.

"You too," he calls back.

I'll need it if I'm going to finish all my orders plus the two he dropped in my lap before noon.

# Chapter 33

### *Liam*

"What do you think is going on at that table?"
I tap a finger against the glass window.

Keats moves to stand next to me. He peers
into the crowded diner. "Which table?"

I point directly to the spot where Athena is
sitting. "That one. The one with the guy with the
messy brown hair and the woman with the gray scarf
around her neck."

"It doesn't take a genius to see that they're
eating lunch." He groans. "I'm jealous. Why are we
not inside chowing down?"

Keats was the one who suggested we meet at
Crispy Biscuit for lunch. We still haven't met up for
pool and beer since we've both been too busy.

"Move it inside." Keats points at the door.
"I'm dying for a club sandwich."

I was in the mood for the BLT until I saw
Athena with another man.

Before I can tell Keats that I've lost my
appetite, his phone rings.

"Go to hell." He sighs.

I huff out a laugh. "You don't even know who
is calling you."

Shaking his head, he chuckles. "Believe me, I know. It's a client. It's *the* client. My number one. He wants to meet today. I told him to hold it together until I'm done having lunch."

"Go." I direct him with a finger in the air.

Fishing his phone out of his pocket, he gives it a glance. "You're sure, Wolf? Because if I'm honest, he's more important that you are at the moment."

"Fuck you," I bite back with a smile. "Get lost."

He raises his hand to wave at someone to our left. "Go inside and pick up something to go."

I glance back at Athena and the suit. He's got his phone in his palm, and her eyes are glued to it. Their foreheads are almost touching as they both lean in to take a look at whatever the fuck is on the screen.

I turn to face Keats. "I'll grab something closer to my office."

"Is she a client?" he questions with a perk of his brow. "You seem surprised to see her here, or is it him?"

"Both."

He doesn't need the details. Athena and I didn't set ground rules. Nothing is stopping her from seeing other men.

"Let's get the hell out of here." He points at a black SUV pulling up to the curb in front of the diner. "That's my ride. We'll drop you off at your office."

I should take the offer, but I need to walk and think. "You go. I'm good."

It's a lie. I'm not good. I'm jealous as fuck. Whoever Athena is having lunch with right now is the luckiest bastard on the planet.

\*\*\*

A canceled appointment has its positives and negatives. I come out of it with extra time to myself. Sometimes I'll spend that working on paperwork, or I'll hit the gym. I've been known to wrangle my mom into meeting me for a coffee.

The downside to a client bailing is worry.

Unless I speak to them directly, there's always the chance that they're having a bad day and can't bring themselves to leave the house or to face their feelings.

Rhys canceled on me when I was at lunch.

His appointment was booked for four p.m., but he called into the office and spoke to Audrey shortly after noon.

He didn't rebook or leave a message.

That's the reason why I sent him a text twenty minutes ago to check in on him.

I'm on my way home for the day, but I'm taking the scenic route, which to me, is a stroll past Grace Church. The architecture of the building is as impressive as its rich history.

My phone chimes, so I dig it out of my pocket just as I'm about to cross the street.

I read the text.

**Rhys:** *Hey! My dad wanted to hang out this afternoon.*

That's the best news I've heard all day.

Rhys's dad has been emotionally spent since his wife died. He hasn't been there for his son or himself.

**Liam:** *Good to hear.*

He responds almost immediately.

**Rhys:** *Give him another week or 2 and I think he'll be up to meeting you on the court.*

I want to do right by Deidre. It was important to her that Gareth work through his pain. This will hopefully help him on that path.

**Liam:** *You name the time and place.*

**Rhys:** *I'll let you know about that but can you fit me in tomorrow? I need to talk something over with you.*

I pop open the calendar app on my phone and scroll through my schedule for tomorrow. It's synced with the office, so whenever Audrey changes anything, I'm up to speed.

**Liam:** *Do you have time at 3 tomorrow?*

I cross the street and navigate my way around the late afternoon rush of people cramming the sidewalks.

I glance down when my phone chimes.

**Rhys:** *I'll be there. Can we talk about a girl? My girl?*

*My girl.*

I read the two words over and over again before I shoot him back a quick response.

**Liam:** *You bet. See you tomorrow at 3.*

I stop in place and stare up at Grace Church. I don't need to ask the heavens above what I should do.

I turn and head back in the direction I just came. I want Athena, and if I have to go through the guy in the suit to get her, I will.

# Chapter 34

*Athena*

My afternoon flew by.

Once I was back at the shop after having lunch with Jeremy, I pitched in to help Leanna finish up our outstanding orders before Al showed up to handle the deliveries and to take his wife home.

A few walk-ins filled my time after that.

Some of the people who live in the neighborhood are becoming regulars. The moment they enter the store, I know what they'll gravitate toward.

I've been adding extra flowers to the bouquets they order. One of the secrets to building my business is creating a foundation of loyal customers.

Word of mouth goes a long way in this city, and if I can create a positive buzz by spoiling a few familiar faces, I'll do it.

One of those faces is in the store now.

Percy Royster comes by once every couple of weeks on his way home from volunteering in the gift shop at a hospital. He picks and chooses what he wants from the containers of flowers in the cooler.

I whip up a bouquet for his wife while we visit.

He's one of my favorite people because he knew the previous owner and always has a gem of a story to tell about her.

Today it was about a morning ten years ago when the supplier delivered enough roses to fill the shop.

An extra zero was added to the order by mistake, so there was a one-day sale on white roses that brought people from all over Manhattan to this little flower shop.

"What do you think?" I hold up a bouquet of peonies.

Clapping his hands together, Percy slides off the stool he's been perched on. "This one will get me an extra kiss tonight, Athena."

I can't contain a smile. "I'll wrap them up."

I glance to the left when the bell chimes over the door. Percy does the same.

Liam takes a step toward us before he stops in place. Adjusting the collar of his blue button-down shirt, he smiles at me before his attention shifts to Percy.

I watch as Liam approaches him from behind. Percy hasn't yet turned his attention back to me.

"Mr. Royster?" Liam questions with a quirk of his lips.

"Yes?"

I stop wrapping the flowers. "You know Percy?"

"He was my fifth-grade history teacher." Liam tilts his head as his gaze settles back on Percy. "You have no idea how much that class changed my life, sir."

Percy looks to me before he turns back to Liam. "I'm sorry. I taught so many kids."

Liam nods. "I don't expect you to remember me, but on the last day of classes before summer, you gave me a book about the early days of New York. I still have it."

"Wait." Percy takes a measured step closer to Liam. Adjusting the glasses on his nose, he gazes up. "Is that Liam Wolf under that beard?"

Liam's hand darts to his chin. "It's me."

Chuckling, Percy extends his hand. "You've changed, son. My, oh my, have you changed."

Liam takes the offered hand and shakes it gently. "You haven't changed at all, sir."

"Bullshit." Percy laughs. "I'm twenty years older. My eyesight isn't as sharp as it once was, and unless you're standing within ten feet of me, don't expect me to hear a word you say."

Liam smiles. "It's good to see you again."

"And you." Percy turns back to me. "I'll get out of the way so you can help this young man find the perfect flowers for his wife."

"I'm not married," Liam is quick to respond.

Our eyes lock for the briefest of moments.

I force myself not to think about what married life with Liam would be like.

We're not even officially dating at this point.

"You'll get there one day. No rush for that." Percy crosses his arms over his chest. "It's good to see you. Who would have thought that I'd run into one of my former students in a floral shop?"

"I'm here often," Liam offers with a glance at me. "This is one of my favorite places in the city."

Percy tosses me a knowing look. "I think I see why."

\*\*\*

I brush past Liam on my way back to my workstation. It's a mess. Between my extended lunch break and the orders I've filled since Leanna left, it looks like a disaster.

"To what do I owe this surprise?" I toss him a smile.

The one he offers back is weak. The corners of his lips barely move. "My last appointment of the day canceled, so I thought I'd drop by to see how your day has been."

"Busy." I sum it up in one word.

Rubbing a hand over his jaw, he exhales. "Look, Athena. I'm just going to come right out and say this."

My head pops up, and the scissors in my hand drop to the table with a thud.

*He's here to dump me.*

Can you dump someone you're only sleeping with? Is that a thing?

I steel myself for his next words. Pasting on a brave face, I stare him straight in the eye. "What is it?"

"I like you," he begins, raking his hand through his hair. "You're sweet, and you're a lot of fun."

I'm that and more, but maybe he hasn't bothered to notice.

I don't offer him back any compliments because I'll reserve those for the next man I sleep with.

*Who am I kidding?* I don't want there to be a next man, at least not yet.

I like Liam. Hanging out with him is fun, and the sex is incredible.

I'm not ready to lose all of that since it just started.

His phone dings. Fishing it out of his pocket, he holds up a finger. "Give me a minute. I need to check what this is."

I'll give him a minute or ten or twenty thousand. I'll give him whatever he needs if it means I have extra time to brace myself for what is about to happen between us.

I watch as his fingers fly over the screen of his phone.

When my phone chimes, I drop my gaze to it hoping that he's not dumping me via text when he's standing less than three feet from where I am.

I open the text message from Jeremy and stare at the attached picture.

He's got Cassidy in his lap, and she's holding tightly to the small bouquet of pink roses I handed him earlier. I tucked a plastic unicorn figurine in the center of it because I knew she'd love the extra surprise.

Tears threaten to flood my eyes.

I love my family and regardless of what happens between Liam and me, I have them. I will always have them.

I rest my phone on the table.

"Who is that?"

I look up to find Liam craning his neck to get a better look at my phone's screen.

I twist it around so he can see the picture. "My brother and my niece."

He studies it carefully before he glances back at me. "That's your brother?"

I nod. "One of them. He's the oldest."

"Your niece is adorable." He swipes his fingers over the screen of his phone. When he turns it toward me, I'm greeted with a picture of two dark-haired little girls. "These are my nieces. Winter and Reese."

I steal a fleeting glance, but I don't want to know about his family. Why show me that when he's on the precipice of walking out of my life forever?

"I'd say it's a three-way tie for the cutest niece in the world." He waves a hand. "I know you're almost ready to shut down for the day, but can you toss together a couple of bouquets like that for them? Complete with a unicorn in each?"

*What's happening?*

How did we go from serious Liam wanting to tell me something to smiling, happy Liam ordering unicorn bouquets for his nieces?

I feel like I'm dangling in the breeze waiting for the next hurricane wind to whip around the corner and knock me on my ass.

I steady my feet on the tile floor and look him straight in the eye. "What did you want to talk about?"

His gaze falls before he levels it back on my face. "We're having fun, right? Do you like hanging out with me?"

*Is that a trick question?*

If he's setting a trap, I'm about to step into the middle of it with both feet. "I'm having a lot of fun. I love hanging out with you."

Relief softens his stance. Rubbing a hand over his beard, he cracks a wide smile. "Good. I just wanted to check-in and make sure we're on the same page."

Doubt tugs at me as I set to work making the bouquets for his nieces. I don't know what the hell just happened between us, but I'll take him at his word.

We're lovers. Nothing more. If I can remember that, I'll be just fine and my heart will be too.

# Chapter 35

## *Liam*

Her brother.

The guy in the suit she was cozying up to at Crispy Biscuit yesterday is her brother.

*What the fuck is wrong with me?*

Athena isn't like the other women I've dated. She's never chased after me or texted me non-stop looking for details about the next time we'll see each other.

She's a successful businesswoman who makes time for me.

After she put the bouquets together yesterday, she handed them off to me after running my credit card.

Just as I was about to suggest we go to dinner, she got a phone call about a consultation for a wedding.

I only heard her side of the conversation, but she excitedly told whoever was on the other end of the call that she had time to meet them at Wild Lilac as soon as they could get there.

Her business is her top priority.

I respect that.

Hell, it impresses the fuck out of me.

All I should be looking for is some one-on-one time with her every week. If I can get that, I'll be a happy man.

I don't know if she can squeeze dating other men into her schedule. When I look at my future, I don't see forever with anyone, so I'm in no position to ask her to be exclusive, but I want it.

Jesus, do I want her to myself.

I clear my throat so Rhys shifts his attention back to me. He's been sitting across from me in my office for the better part of thirty minutes, but his focus has primarily been on his phone.

He's been texting the girl he told me about as soon as he sat his ass down in the chair.

They go to school together, but their bond started years ago when they met at a party in middle school.

His mom's death set a fire under both of them, so they're dating now.

I don't know if he came here looking for reassurance that it's all right for him to dive into this now. He hasn't said more than a few words to me, so I get the ball rolling because I'll need to send him on his way before my next appointment arrives.

"What's she like?" I quiz with a half-smile.

"Nothing like mom," he bounces back. "She's a free spirit."

The comparison to his mom right out of the gate is enough to warrant a red flag. I press for more. "Your mom wasn't a free spirit?"

I didn't know Deidre before she was diagnosed with cancer. The woman I met with was somber but compassionate. She had tunnel vision because of the circumstances she was facing. Everything revolved around her son and her husband and their futures after she died.

"She was when I was a kid." He picks at a thread on his torn jeans. "As I got older, she got more serious."

Facing death will do that to a person.

"She knew Jailyn." His face brightens with the mention of his girlfriend's name. "She liked her but thought she wasn't taking advantage of her full potential."

Spoken like any parent who wants the best for their child as they're facing the end of their life.

"I'm not marrying her tomorrow." He chuckles, patting the center of his chest with his pointer finger. "But she helps me forget the pain in here."

If he needs Jailyn to distract him from the pain, that works, as long as he still makes a point of coming to see me.

"How are you making out with convincing your dad to meet me on the basketball court?"

I'm making progress with Rhys, but I want to meet Gareth. It was important to his wife that I make an effort to help her family.

"Give him another couple of weeks." He shrugs. "He's working his way up to it."

I'll let it sit for now.

"I need to go." He pushes to his feet. "Jailyn wants to meet for a coffee."

Standing, I rest a hand on his shoulder. "I like the red hair, Rhys. You'll call if you need anything?"

"You're number two on my speed dial." He waves his phone in front of my face. "I'll catch you next week, Wolf."

I follow him out of my office and watch as he sprints to the double glass doors. He pushes a finger into the elevator call button over and over.

He may be burying his pain beneath his desire for a woman, but I can't fault him for that. I'm guilty of the same.

# Chapter 36

*Athena*

I stand back and look over the bouquet in his hands.

"You're killing me here." Liam presses a hand over the left side of his chest. "This has to be a seven, lilac. Admit that I'm improving."

Sighing, I gaze up at his handsome face. "This may be your worst attempt yet."

Keeping a straight face, I cluck my tongue.

"What the hell?" he spits out in a low tone. "You're joking, right? Take another look."

*I am joking.*

I didn't know if Liam would show up at my drop-in class tonight. I smiled when I saw him stroll in wearing jeans and the same NYPD T-shirt he had on the other night.

All of the other students in the class did a double take. Word must have spread that my class offers not only a great deal on beginner flower designing but a hot male student to gawk at.

I had double the number of people crammed into the shop tonight than I did the first night I offered the class.

They've all since left with their bouquets in hand. Some were spectacular. Others weren't as great, but everyone had fun tonight.

Drawing in a deep breath, I touch the edge of one of the peonies in his bouquet. "I'm going to give this one a solid six-and-a-half."

"Fuck," he drawls out slowly. "You're tough."

Nodding, I half-shrug. "Would you rather I not be honest with you?"

He narrows his blue eyes. "I want you always to be honest with me."

I want the same from him. I've never understood the purpose of hiding behind an outright lie. If we're going to keep hanging out with each other, we need to tell it like it is.

"I'm honestly telling you that this bouquet is better than the last one you made."

A smile ghosts his mouth. "That's all I wanted to hear."

I glance at the table and the tattered remains of the flowers that my students left behind.

It's going to take me at least an hour to tidy the shop. The smart thing to do would be to tackle that job tonight, but I'd much rather spend that time with the man standing in front of me.

"Are we cleaning that mess up?" Liam starts to move around me headed straight for the table.

I stop him with a hand to his forearm. "I'll take care of it tomorrow."

His gaze scans my face. I see a question there, but before he can ask, his lips are on mine.

\*\*\*

The sight of Liam Wolf naked from behind is incredible.

I told him I had to use the washroom as soon as we got to his apartment. I didn't have to do anything but give myself a pep talk in his bathroom mirror.

This time it wasn't about encouraging myself to find the nerve to sleep with him.

I want that. It's all I wanted when we kissed in the narrow elevator on our way up to his apartment.

We walked part of the way here before a thunderstorm rolled over the city. Once the wind picked up, we ran to the nearest subway stop.

The blouse I was wearing was sprinkled with wet spots from the rain. Liam's T-shirt was too. He yanked it off as soon as we were inside his apartment. I watched as he tugged off his boots and socks.

Sometime between when I went into the washroom, and now he's lost the rest of his clothing.

I'm only wearing my underwear.

It's nothing special.

It's a matching white cotton bra and panty.

"I see you," he says quietly.

I catch his gaze in the reflection of the glass. "I see you too."

He spins around and drops his hands to his hips.

*Dear God.*

"How is it possible that you were in this city, and I never knew?" He takes a measured step closer to me. "I must have walked past Wild Lilac a dozen times in the past year, and yet I didn't know."

With shaking hands, I take a step toward him. "I never knew you were in this city either."

179

He rakes me from head-to-toe. "The pull is so strong now. When I leave here in the morning, I have to fight against the urge to go to your store. On my lunch break, I think about heading uptown to see you. If I knew where you lived, I'd camp out on your stoop every night until you came home."

"I don't have a stoop," I say with another tentative step forward. "I live in a walkup."

"I want to see it." He rakes a hand through his hair. "Do you know how hard it is to imagine you in bed at night when I've never seen your bed?"

I laugh to veil my nerves. "You can come over sometime."

"Soon," he adds. "I want to see it soon."

If any other man pushed me in this way, I'd tell him to back off, but I want Liam in my home. I want him to fall asleep on my sheets so that I'll smell him there the next night and the night after that.

"Soon," I repeat as I take a final step until I'm in front of him.

"You know how grateful I am that I met you, right?" He reaches forward to cup my cheek in his palm. "I'm so damn lucky that I know you."

Inching forward, I rest my hands on his chest. "I'm damn lucky too."

He brushes his thumb over my bottom lip. "Come to bed with me, lilac."

I lean forward when he presses his mouth to mine. The almost silent "*yes, please*," that falls from my mouth gets lost in our kiss.

# Chapter 37

*Liam*

Sometimes I fear that I might break Athena in two.

It was that way tonight when I ate her to two orgasms. I tugged her legs apart after I stripped her panties off.

She moaned as I devoured her pussy. The taste is incredible. The slickness against my mouth was enough to drive my hips into the mattress over and over again as I fucked her with my tongue.

When she came the second time, she tore her fingers through my hair.

The burst of pain was almost too much.

I sheathed my cock and took her in one smooth thrust.

She held onto me as I fucked her hard, my thrusts driving the headboard into the wall.

I came after she did a second time, but it's still not enough.

It will never be enough with her.

I'll always want more.

"Liam," she whispers my name with her eyes closed. "Am I dreaming?"

The sound of the rain against the window lulled her to sleep after I wrapped a blanket around her.

I stayed awake because life is as beautiful as it is cruel.

I didn't want to fall in love, yet here I am.

I can deny it all the fuck I want to, but dammit my heart. It's coming apart in threads of want and need and the only time it feels whole is when I'm looking into Athena's eyes, or when I hear her voice, or when her hands touch my skin.

"Lilac," I whisper back with my lips against her pink cheek. "You're not dreaming."

"You're real." She pops open one eye just a crack. "How can a man like you be real?"

I'm not without my faults, or without my broken and battered pieces.

I'm far from fucking perfect, but if given a chance, I'd do everything in my power to make her life a dream come true.

I close my eyes against the assault of reality that is punching me straight in the gut.

I don't get to have that with her.

I rest my forehead against the side of her face. "I want to taste you again."

I feel the curve of her lips as they rise into a smile. "Can I tell you a secret?"

*Tell me every single last one of them so I can save them to memory and guard them with my heart.*

"Tell me."

Her eyes stay closed. "I came twice when you had your mouth on me."

I felt it. I wanted another, but she pushed my head away.

"Do you want to make it three times?" I hear the note of desperation in my question. She has to hear it too. I don't give a fuck. I want her. Why try and hide that from her?

"I thought maybe…"

I wait, but nothing follows, so I reach for her breast. I give her right nipple a pinch. "Finish, Athena. You thought maybe what?"

Her mouth opens slightly before a jagged exhale escapes her. "I've never put my mouth on a man before in that way."

My dick hardens at the thought of my cock being the first to part those lips. "You want to suck me off."

Why mince words when we're talking about her blowing me?

She nods. "I want to try."

I push back the blanket to expose my throbbing dick. "It's all yours, lilac."

When her eyes open, the heat in her gaze pierces through me. "Be patient with me. This is new for me."

*It's new for me too.*

I'm in bed with a woman I'm falling in love with. I'm about to feel her lips circling my cock.

If this isn't as good as it gets, I don't know what the hell is.

I suck in a heady breath as she trails her long hair over my chest toward my stomach.

When her fingers reach my cock, I rest a hand on her shoulder and close my eyes.

I'll never forget this moment or this woman for as long as I live.

# Chapter 38

## *Athena*

"How would you rate my performance on a scale of one to ten?" I try to keep from smiling as I stare down at his naked body. He's sprawled on his back in the middle of his bed.

"You're fucking joking."

I push against his bicep. "Liam."

"Athena." He looks over at me. "Give me a minute to find my bearings."

"That must mean that it was better than a five." I fall onto the mattress next to him.

I know it was better than a five. From the way he came in my mouth, I think it was close to a ten.

I couldn't handle all of him, but I took what I could.

He tried to let me be in control, but his restraint broke, and his hands got lost in my hair as he fucked my mouth. It was slow at first, but then his thrusts came faster and harder until he exploded.

He pulled out after the first burst of his release hit my tongue. He shot the rest on his stomach.

I trailed my tongue through it as he watched with wide eyes and his mouth hanging open.

"Christ. I can't breathe." He presses a hand against the left side of his chest. "Did my heart stop?"

I move to rest my ear against his chest. "It's beating strong inside of there. Thump, thump, thump."

A roar of laughter flows through him, vibrating his body under mine. "I guarantee it's not that quiet."

I inch away from his chest so I can look into his face. "Your heartbeat is fine. You're going to live."

His brow knits. "Is that your professional opinion as the best florist in Manhattan?"

"In all of New York City," I correct him. "I set my sights high."

"As you should." He trails a finger over my forehead. "That was perfect. Everything about what you just did was utter perfection."

I believe him.

My gaze wanders to the window and the darkness beyond. It's late. I should leave. My plan wasn't to stay over. I have to be at the shop early for another large delivery.

"Don't say it." He groans out the words. "You're thinking about taking off."

Speechless, I glance at him. How the hell does he know that?

"I can see the wheels churning behind those beautiful baby blues." He looks me straight in the eyes. "You're thinking about going home to sleep so you can get an early start on your day tomorrow."

I straighten my legs, brushing my toes against his calf. "Business has picked up lately."

He jerks a thumb over his shoulder to where his phone is sitting on the nightstand. "I'll set the alarm for an hour before you want to go to work. I can take you home, see your place, and give you a shower before I walk you to Wild Lilac."

It's a plan with one major flaw.

Shaking my head, I exhale. "My shower is tiny. We both can't fit in there."

That lures a smile to his mouth. "You're sure?"

"My apartment is Athena-sized, not giant-sized."

"Giant-sized." He tosses my words back with a lift of both of his brows. "I admit I'm tall, but I'm no giant, lilac."

I pick at a loose thread on the pillowcase next to me. "We can't both fit in my shower."

"We'll shower here before we go to your place." He glances at the door that leads to the hallway. "I'll even make you a coffee before we head out in the morning."

It's all so tempting. It's not just the idea of showering with him, but the comfort of spending the night wrapped in his arms while the rain beats down on the city.

"I'll stay." I slide into place next to him. "Set the alarm for five."

"I'm setting it for four-thirty," he counters. "I need an extra thirty minutes in the morning with you."

Before I think it through, I ask a question. "For what?"

He slides his hand up my thigh. "For this."

***

186

I wake before the alarm sounds. It's that way every morning. I set the alarm on my phone before I go to bed most nights, but my scattered thoughts push through my peaceful dreams, and I wake up at least an hour before I want to.

I won't complain about not getting much sleep in Liam's bed.

I reach for him, but all my hand finds is the cold sheet where he was before I fell asleep.

He held me against his chest until I drifted off.

He was telling me about the Empire State Building and the workers who put in time crafting one of the most iconic buildings in New York City.

"Liam," I say his name quietly as I survey the room.

He's not in here, but there is a light trailing down the hallway from the main living area.

My breath catches in my throat when my bare feet hit the cold hardwood floor.

Bundling a blanket around me, I push to stand.

He might have gone to fetch a glass of water or to use the washroom, but I want to surprise him by tossing the blanket aside to reveal my body underneath.

I know it will earn me at least a smile and those are like gold to me.

His entire face lights up when happiness settles there.

As soon as I peer out of the bedroom door, I spot him. He's standing in silence, staring at a wall of pictures. I've glanced at them briefly each time I've been here. I know the one in the center with all of the people at a restaurant has to be a photo of his family.

There are also pictures of him when he was a kid and one from his high school graduation.

I move forward two steps and turn to face him.

He's wearing dark sweatpants and nothing else. His right fist is knotted in the center of his chest. I can only see his profile, but I see pain there. It's evident in the stern set of his jaw and the furrow of his brow.

I feel like I'm interrupting something even though he's alone.

I move slightly, causing the bottom of the blanket to brush against the floor.

That's enough to turn him in my direction.

"You're awake?" he asks with a grin. "I thought you'd sleep straight through until morning."

Stepping closer to him, I study his face. "Are you all right?"

A curt nod is the only reply I get.

I could pry for more, but whatever brought him to this spot isn't something he wants to share right now.

He pins his gaze to my bare shoulder as the blanket starts to slide down my body. "It's early, but do you want to join me in my shower?"

Silently, I give the lightweight blanket a shove revealing myself to him.

He stalks toward me with his arms outstretched. "Bed first. Shower after."

He heaves me up and over his shoulder in one fluid movement.

When I scream in glee, he rewards me with a light tap of his palm on my ass.

"Save those sounds for when I'm inside of you." He growls as he carries me over the threshold and into his bedroom.

# Chapter 39

*Athena*

I twist the locket around my neck in a circle as I take in the massive delivery that I just signed for.

*How is this my life?*

My business has reached new heights the past few weeks, and my heart is soaring just as high in my chest.

I'm in love with Liam Wolf.

I don't need to ask anyone what love feels like anymore because I'm experiencing it firsthand.

I pop open the locket and stare at the pictures of the man and the woman.

The missing pieces of my past don't matter as much anymore. I didn't know what my future looked like until now, so the past was what I clung to.

A rap on the shop door turns me right around.

I glance down at my phone.

It's not even seven a.m. yet. I know it can't be Liam. He took a call just as we were about to leave my apartment.

He joked with a man named Keats about a missed lunch. I heard him agree to meet him for breakfast today. He asked if I wanted to go with him, but I needed to get here to meet the deliveryman and start on today's orders.

I inch my way closer to the door until I see my brother peering in.

I toss him a wave and a smile.

He throws me back a big grin before he points at the door handle.

I rush over to unlock it.

"Why the hell do you come to work at the crack of dawn?" Jeremy gathers me into his arms. "I was passing by and saw the lights were on."

"You were passing by?" I ask with a heavy dose of skepticism lacing my tone.

Brushing a hand over the arm of his black suit jacket, he huffs out a laugh. "I stopped by your apartment last night. You weren't there."

I know that his concern is grounded in love. My older brother has always looked out for me. When I was in high school, I was asked to the senior prom. Jeremy insisted on meeting the guy before he agreed to take me to buy a dress.

He wasn't my dream prom date by any means, but he handled himself well during Jeremy's interrogation.

"I was out."

"Smartass." He levels the words at me with a wink. "I just want to know if his intentions are honorable, Athena."

"You might want to jump into this century, Jer." I roll my eyes before I lower my voice to mimic his. "Were your intentions honorable when you spent the night in Vegas with Linny? Didn't you two meet for the first time that day?"

A sheepish grin plays on his lips. "Touché."

"Did you come down here before daybreak to check up on me?"

His gaze falls to the locket hanging around my neck. Jeremy knows the story. He understands that I've wanted to patch together my past for years.

"I came here because I love my sister." He crosses his arms over his chest. "Why don't you invite him to have dinner with us on your birthday?"

That's soon. It feels too soon to introduce Liam to my family.

"That deer in the headlight look you've got going on is telling me something." He taps his chin. "If he's important to you, Athena, we want to meet him."

I'm touched that he recognizes that Liam isn't like the other men I've dated.

"Give it some thought." He inches around me headed toward the coolers. "If you feel up to it, there will be an extra chair at our table at Nova for him."

Nova is the restaurant we always go to when one of us is celebrating a birthday. It's a family tradition. Jeremy has never offered to add an extra chair for anyone before.

I trail behind him as he heads straight for my workstation. "I'll think about it."

He stops mid-step to turn and face me. "I'll be on my best behavior. I can't say the same for my daughter."

I laugh as I round him. "Speaking of Cass, I take it you want a little something to surprise her with when you go back home to tell Linny about this conversation?"

He huffs out a laugh. "She was set to come, but Cass wasn't having it. She wanted her mama this morning."

I slide open the door of the cooler and tug two pink roses out of a large bucket. I shove them into his hand. "Tell Linny I love her. Cass too."

He arches a brow. "Me too?"

Pushing to my tiptoes, I kiss his cheek. "You too."

\*\*\*

As I lock the door of the shop, a hand on my shoulder spins me around fast. I have my key in my hand to use for protection if need be. It's a trick my mom taught me when I was a kid. I was responsible for getting my younger brothers home from school, so I had a key in my pocket.

We lived in a rental house in upstate New York back then.

We had enough land that we could run through the field and get lost beneath the tall grass if we crouched down.

I'd spend hours chasing Breccan and Zach under the sunshine.

That was our home for less than three months, but I still consider it one of the best places in the world.

Audrey's hands dart in the air in surrender. "It's just me."

I let out a giggle. I had waited an extra thirty minutes past closing time for her to show up to give final approval on the flowers for her wedding. I texted her twice to ask if she wanted to reschedule, but I didn't get a reply, so I sent one final message telling her that she could stop by the shop before work tomorrow.

Hurrying to unlock the door, I apologize. "I'm sorry. You startled me."

She brushes past me when I motion for her to step inside first. "A woman can't be too careful in this city. You're prepared in the event of an emergency. I am too."

She pats the outside of the designer bag slung over her forearm.

I don't ask what she has in there to fend off a would-be-attacker. Instead, I flick the overhead lights back on and lock the door behind us.

"I just saw your text messages now." She dips her chin toward the phone in her hand. "I was talking to my fiancé on my way over. Jay. His name is Jay. He's stopping by to check out the flowers. That's not a problem, is it?"

Why would it be?

I've only ever had amazing experiences when men have joined their fiancées to choose the flowers for their wedding. It's always a treat for me because I get a feel for the unique dynamic of the couple. That insight is helpful when it comes to suggesting the style of arrangements for the ceremony.

I smile. "It's not a problem at all."

Audrey's gaze leaps over my shoulder to the door just as I hear a faint rap on it. "Speak of the sexy devil. There he is."

I smile at her choice of words. She's head over heels for her future husband.

I unlock the glass door and swing it open to find a man with salt and pepper hair and blue eyes hidden behind black-rimmed eyeglasses. "Hi. I'm Athena. You must be Jay. Welcome to Wild Lilac."

# Chapter 40

## *Liam*

Just as I round the corner to sprint to Wild Lilac, I spot Athena leaving the shop with Audrey and her fiancé.

*What the hell?*

When I saw Audrey an hour ago, she was racing out of the office even though she was scheduled to work the late shift with me.

She's worked for Winola for years. I know they go way back. It's one of the reasons Audrey can take off early when the need arises. Her job is secure. There's no way in hell that Winola would ever send Audrey packing.

Audrey spots me first out of the corner of her eye. Her hand rises in the air in an animated greeting. "Wolf! What are you doing here?"

I have no idea if Athena wants Audrey to know we're involved, so I pause to let her take the lead on this one.

She does so seamlessly. "Liam is here to pick up bouquets for his nieces."

I'll go with that.

"You're late." Audrey drums her fingertips over my chest. "We were all late. Athena should have shut down the store an hour ago."

That might be true, but I was holding out hope that I'd catch her before she took off for the night.

I want to walk her home so I can spend the night with her.

Her apartment is cramped, and I can already tell that my feet will hang off the end of the bed, but I want to be next to her when I fall asleep tonight.

"Wolf." Jay extends a hand to me. "It's good to see you again."

I can say the same. Jay stops by to drop off lunch for the office a couple of times a month. He works at Axel Tribeca as a chef. It's an upscale place that I don't ordinarily frequent, but the food is damn good.

I give his hand a firm shake.

"We're headed to the restaurant to grab a bite." His gaze volleys between Athena and me. "You two are welcome to join us."

"Jay is the best chef in the city." Audrey turns her full attention to Athena. "He works at Axel Tribeca. You should come with us. The food is seriously out of this world."

Athena glances down at the black sweater and dark jeans she's wearing. "I don't think I'm dressed for…"

"Nonsense," Audrey interjects with a light swat at Athena's ponytail. "You're beautiful."

Athena looks to me. I toss her a shrug because I'll go wherever she's inclined to. We can grab some food with Audrey and Jay and still have time alone at her place.

"Liam's flowers," Athena says with a sigh. "I should get those for him to give to his nieces."

Audrey waves her wrist in the air showing off a gold watch. "They're in bed by now. Wolf's first appointment isn't until noon. He can stop by here in the morning, pick up the bouquets and surprise Winter and Reese."

She's right. I talked to my brother, Nicholas, on my way here. He had just finished reading a bedtime story to his daughters. They get up at the crack of dawn, so it's lights out early for the two of them.

Athena and I aren't going to win this battle. She must sense it too because she pipes up. "I'd love to join the two of you for dinner."

"I'm in too," I add quickly.

I'm not letting this woman out of my sight tonight. If I have to sit through a quick meal before I feast on her, I'll do it.

*** 

"What did you think of the food?" I ask Athena as we set off down the sidewalk after leaving Axel Tribeca.

I offered to walk her to the subway after she announced that she needed to call it a night.

We spent two hours listening to every detail of Audrey and Jay's upcoming wedding. When Jay managed to get a few words in, he focused them on Athena.

He was interested in her work, and she was happy to talk about it.

She gained a new customer tonight.

"On a scale of one to ten, it was one million." She tosses me a smile. "That lobster thing in the sauce...wow. I mean, just wow. It was the best part."

I admit it was good, but the best part was sitting across a square table from her and watching her every move.

I tried to keep my focus on the conversation, but it was near impossible. Athena is breathtaking.

"Jay seems nice," she remarks as we wait to cross the street. "He told me I could come by one day when he's working to check out the kitchen of the restaurant."

I watched her face light up when he offered the invitation. "You'll take him up on that, right?"

"Of course, I will." She tugs on the sleeve of my blue button-down shirt once the light changes. "I've already seen the kitchen, though."

I huff out a laugh. "You've already seen the kitchen of Axel Tribeca?"

She turns to look up at me. "Where do you think all those beautiful floral arrangements in the restaurant come from?"

I crack a smile. "You?"

"Me," she sounds back with a nod of her head. "I convinced Hunter Reynolds, the owner, to sign a contract with me six months ago. Wild Lilac supplies all the fresh flowers for his restaurants in Manhattan."

It's impressive. Damn, this woman is fearless.

"You blow me away." I reach for her hand. "I want to be more like you."

That raises her brows. "You want to be more like me? Why?"

"You don't let anything get in your way." I brush a hand over her cheek. "If you want something, you go for it."

Her eyes lock on mine. "I want something now."

*I hope to fuck I'm it.*

198

"What do you want, lilac?"

Her thumb jerks to the right. "Get on the subway with me, and I'll show you."

# Chapter 41

## *Athena*

I can't move.

*Literally.*

Liam has me pinned to my bed. Both of my wrists are in one of his hands above my head. He's on top of me, balancing his full weight on his palm. It's pressed into the mattress next to my shoulder.

My legs are pushed apart by the width of his hips.

Every inch of my skin is sensitive from his touch. He kissed, licked, and fucked me until I lost my breath.

Judging by the brush of his sheathed cock against my core, he's hard as nails again.

"Jesus, you're beautiful." The words fall from his mouth in a whispered rush. "I think I could spend the rest of my life staring at you non-stop, and I'd still want more."

Tears threaten to fill my eyes, but I bite them back with a heavy swallow.

I study his face.

I can't tell if I'm looking at a man who is falling just as hard for me as I am for him, or if he's speaking out of intense desire.

Maybe it's both?

He presses his lips to my collarbone. "Tell me who is inside this locket around your neck."

"*I don't know.*" I mouth the words because I can't give them a voice.

I'm embarrassed that the piece of jewelry means more to me than almost anything on this earth.

He moves slightly, dropping kisses on the skin of my neck. "Say it's not your last boyfriend."

I let out a burst of laughter. "It's not."

His lips brush the corner of my mouth before he rests his cheek against mine. "He was a fool to let you go, lilac."

I dumped him.

It wasn't working. In addition to the sex being average, he couldn't wrap his head around the fact that I wanted to start my own business.

He didn't think I had the experience I needed to succeed.

I proved him wrong.

Talking about an ex while I'm in bed with my current lover is a big no-no to me.

I shift under him, trying to brush my pussy against his cock.

The expression on his face morphs the second he feels my movements. "You want me."

I love that there's no doubt in his voice or his body.

He nudges himself closer to me, parting my folds with his erection.

"I want you," I whisper. "So much, Liam."

His hand slides under my thigh. "Being inside of you is almost too much."

I know the feeling. When he's fucking me, everything slips away but the two of us.

In one swift movement, my ass is in his hand, and he's pressing inside of me. My body adjusts to his cock with each slide forward.

"You'll tell me if I hurt you."

I nod, my eyes shut from the depth of the pleasure. It's already so good. "It doesn't hurt."

"I'll never hurt you." He grunts when he pushes deeper. "I will never hurt you."

I roll my hips with each drive of his cock.

"Please never hurt me," I whisper into the skin of his shoulder as he buries his face in my neck, pumping into me faster and deeper with each thrust.

\*\*\*

I wake to the sound of Liam's voice.

It takes me a second to realize that we're in my apartment. My body is still tingling from our lovemaking.

I tug the blanket up to my neck to fend off the cold.

Early fall in Manhattan boasts warm days, but there's a bite in the air once the sun drops.

"You're sure he's up to it?"

I crane my neck to look in the direction of Liam's voice. He's in my bathroom. The door doesn't shut completely. When I first moved in, Jeremy promised that he'd have someone come by to remedy that, but he must have forgotten.

I haven't reminded him because I live alone, and a non-closing door doesn't bother me.

"We'll do it this week, Rhys," he says in a low tone. "Your mom would be proud of you for making this happen."

I close my eyes when silence follows.

"You didn't wake me." His voice softens. "But, I'm about to get into bed."

The sound of the door creaking cracks open one of my eyelids.

I glance over to see him standing in the doorway, completely nude.

"I told you that I'm here for you twenty-four, seven." His bare feet pad against the hardwood as he approaches the bed. "You need me, you call. Alright?"

When I know he's close enough to see me, I smile.

I'm rewarded with a grin. "I'll talk to you soon, Rhys."

As soon as the words leave his lips, the phone is on the foot of the bed, and Liam is crawling over me.

"I wasn't trying to hear that." I turn on my side to face him.

"He's lost since his mom died." He circles my waist with his arm, tugging me closer. "We've formed a bond. I want him to know I'm always around if he needs me."

Cradling his face in my hands, I press a kiss to his mouth. "You're a good man."

"I'm a lucky man," he counters. "I'm in bed with the most beautiful woman I've ever known."

"Will you fall asleep now?" I ask, hoping that he'll say *no*.

He gently pushes me onto my back before he slides down my body to settle between my legs. "This first, lilac. Another taste, and then I'll dream about you."

# Chapter 42

### *Athena*

I made it to Wild Lilac with time to spare before my daily delivery arrived.

I have no idea how I pulled that off. I didn't want to leave the bed or Liam's arms, but duty called, so I showered first and got dressed while he watched my every move.

I let him help button up my blouse and tie my hair back.

He was gentle and eager, taking time to tell me how much he admired me.

Once he showered, we walked to the shop hand-in-hand, stopping to talk to the bodega owner and to inhale the scent of freshly baked bread before he kissed me goodbye and left.

"Good morning!"

I crane my neck to see Leanna march into the store with a cup of tea in each hand.

I rush toward her to offer help since she's balancing a large tote bag on one shoulder.

"I'll take these." I reach for the cups.

"Thank you," she replies with a wink. "They always offer a tray, and I always decline. Why?"

Laughing, I set the cups down on the checkout counter. "You have a system that works. Why mess with that?"

"I'm tempting fate with my system." She waves a hand at me. "One wrong move and I'll end up with third degree burns. Tomorrow I'm getting a tray unless you want to meet me there tomorrow."

She lost me after the first *tomorrow*. "Meet you where?"

Rolling her eyes, she lets out a giggle. "At the café two blocks over."

I still feel like I'm fumbling around in the dark, so I take a sip of tea with the hope that she'll keep talking. I need her to fill in the blanks.

"I've seen your friend there twice." Leanna grabs the other cup of tea. Popping open the plastic lid, she blows on the hot liquid.

Leanna considers everyone who walks through Wild Lilac's doors a friend. "Which friend?"

"The hot guy who bought you pizza." She fans herself with her hand. "He looks just as hot in the morning when he's drinking coffee."

*She should see him naked in bed.*

"He was with a gorgeous man the other day." She wiggles both brows. "Today, it's a beautiful woman."

Jealousy spears through me even though I have no idea who Liam is with.

"If you hurry, I think you could catch up to him and say *hi*." She waves her fingers at me. "Don't let that slip through your grasp, Athena."

Setting my shoulders back, I suck in a deep breath. Liam doesn't strike me as the type of man who rolls out of bed with one woman to meet another for coffee. Besides, if he went to the café right after he left me here, he's already been there for close to two hours.

Putting faith in anyone other than the people closest to me isn't easy, but I trust Liam. I shake off the envy and think about how he looked at me when he kissed me goodbye this morning.

"I'm going to stay right where I am and enjoy this tea with you."

Tapping the side of her cup against mine, she smiles. "Cheers to that! Let's get to work."

\*\*\*

Even though he didn't mention it this morning, I was hoping that Liam would appear for my drop-in flower arranging class.

He was a no show.

I wasn't the only person disappointed by that.

At least half of the women in the shop asked where he was. I shrugged and told them that I had no idea since that's the truth.

I was able to keep their focus on the bouquets in front of them.

Everyone left with a pretty bunch of flowers and a smile. I can't complain about that.

I gaze out the window of the shop as I ready to lock up for the night.

People file past on their way down the sidewalk. Cars whiz by on the street.

Manhattan is never quiet, but at a moment like this, when I'm separated from its frenetic energy by two panes of glass, I feel as though I'm somewhere else.

As a little girl, I always imagined I'd live in a place with lots of green grass and apple trees.

I saw myself as a mom to a son and a daughter and married to a man who would cherish me always.

I wanted what my mother never had.

Stability.

Focus.

Hope.

I twist around to look at my shop. I take in the leaves scattered on the floor under the table and the empty vases that my students used to hold their bouquets before they wrapped them in lilac paper and took them home.

Tears well in the corners of my eyes.

This is better than any dream I ever had when I was a kid, and Liam Wolf is better than the prince charming I imagined I'd marry one day.

I want this to be my life, always. I want Liam to be part of my life forever.

I hope he feels the same way about me.

# Chapter 43

*Liam*

This wasn't how I imagined I'd be spending my night.

I had a master plan that included taking one of my sisters-in-law to meet the woman I'm falling in love with.

Tilly, Sebastian's wife, sent me a text early this morning to see if I was around to have coffee with her.

She works at a vet clinic a few blocks from Wild Lilac, so I suggested the café that I'd met Keats at.

Tilly showed up looking green around the edges.

Morning sickness is kicking her ass, so I bought her an herbal tea and plopped myself down at a table across from her.

My first appointment wasn't until noon, and her shift didn't start until ten, so we talked.

Actually, Tilly talked.

We've become close since she married my oldest brother. She's as much a sister to me as Nikita is. Sophia, Nicholas's wife, is too.

I'm damn lucky to have so many strong women in my life.

By the time Tilly had confessed all of her fears about being a first-time mom, she had to leave for work.

I didn't have a chance to talk about Athena with her, so I invited her to the flower arranging class with me.

She was in until I was out.

Work kept me away from Wild Lilac.

I'm still at my office, waiting for a woman who lost her sister two months ago. We've been working through the guilt she's experiencing. They were supposed to take a Caribbean cruise together, but an argument kept one of them on dry land.

The other had a fatal heart attack on the third day of her trip.

"I'm taking off." Audrey taps the open door of my office. "I wanted to say that it was fun hanging out with you last night."

I offer a smile in response because I don't remember much about dinner at Axel Tribeca other than how Athena looked.

Taking a step into my office, Audrey lowers her gaze. "Athena's situation is tragic, isn't it?"

That perks both my brows. "Tragic? How so?"

"Her mom and her step-dad." She juts out her chin. "I didn't want to say anything to her about it, but damn that's a heavy load for a young woman to carry around with her for the rest of her life."

*What the actual fuck is she talking about?*

I don't view Google as an ally when it comes to dating. I've never searched online for insider information on any of the women I've been involved with.

If there's something about them they want me to know, I trust they'll share it.

Audrey crosses her arms over her chest. "I don't personally know anyone who lost their life savings to those two, but plenty of people in this city were robbed blind by Simone Millett and her husband. It takes courage for Athena to hold her head up high and walk around this city. I don't think I could do it if I were her."

*The sins of the parent should never be a burden for their child.*

My dad said those words to my siblings and me when he was shot in the leg in the line of duty. I went to school with the kid of the man who pulled the trigger.

It was my first tangible lesson in the power of forgiveness.

Rising to my feet, I adjust the buckle of my belt. "Athena is an incredible woman. She's her own person. I never judge someone on the actions of another."

Audrey steps back. "I don't either, Wolf."

The lines between judgment and gossip are blurry to some, including Audrey.

Ending this conversation now is what I need, so I do it. "I'll see you tomorrow."

She takes the hint and turns to walk away. "Goodnight, Wolf."

I wish to fuck I was the one leaving right now so I could find Athena and wrap her in my arms. All I want to do is protect her.

***

A two-hour appointment wasn't what I planned on, but it's what was needed.

Grief works on its own schedule. Sometimes when a person opens up for the first time about loss, their feelings can't be shut down.

That's what I experienced tonight as I sat with the woman who lost her sister on the cruise ship.

She needed to let everything out.

I listened, I advised, but most of all, I applauded her for taking the time to come and see me.

We'll meet again next week.

She'll heal. The guilt will linger for as long as it needs to, but she'll move through this. She's determined to make the most of the rest of her life in honor of her sister.

I fall into one of the chairs in the waiting room after locking the doors of the Dehaven Center.

Scrolling through my messages, I spot one from Rhys.

**Rhys:** *My dad's ready to take you on, Wolf. Name the time, and we'll bring the basketball.*

I'll look through my schedule in the morning to see when I can fit that in. I want it to happen as soon as possible. Deidre made me promise I'd do my best to help her family.

I won't let her down.

I scroll until I find a string of messages from Athena sent less than an hour ago.

**Athena:** *Did you know that the Statue of Liberty was delivered in over 300 pieces?*

I laugh aloud when I read her next message.

**Athena:** *Of course, you know that. You know EVERYTHING about this city.*

I tap through to the next message she sent ten minutes later.

**Athena:** *I'm falling asleep. Dream about me tonight, Liam.*

I type out a response and press send.
**Liam:** *I do every night, lilac. Sweet dreams.*

# Chapter 44

*Athena*

Corporate clients are the foundation I'm trying to build on. I have contracts with a bridal shop, several restaurants, and a dental office. Now, I'm working on landing a deal to supply four large arrangements a week to Whispers of Grace.

It's a jewelry store owned by one of Linny's long-time clients, Ivy Marlow-Walker.

She's a designer who has built an empire from the ground up.

Linny loves telling me the story of how Ivy started her business in the spare room of her apartment when she was my age.

That wasn't that long ago, but now, Ivy is living her dream.

A new collection of her necklaces will be featured in the gift bags for one of the biggest award shows of the season.

Linny had a hand in that.

I'm proud of her, and I'm excited that she invited me along to meet Ivy this morning at her boutique.

"Ivy is going to love those." Linny touches her fingertips to one of the daisies in my hand. "Daisies are her absolute favorite."

I asked so I could be sure that I came prepared.

Linny has already mentioned Wild Lilac to Ivy, and she expressed some interest, so I'm here to seal the deal.

I have a navy blue dress on and the butterfly earrings that Linny gave me for my birthday a year ago. Ivy is the designer. I cried when I opened the gift-wrap to find the box from Whispers of Grace.

I rarely wear the earrings because I'm terrified that I'll lose one.

I suck in a deep breath when Linny pulls open the door to the quaint jewelry shop in SoHo.

A petite woman with long blonde hair gazes in our direction. A smile lights up her face. "Linny!"

She races over. The pretty pink dress she's wearing sways as she walks.

I stand to the side as she throws her arms around Linny. "Can you believe it? We're going to Hollywood!"

I watch my sister-in-law as she tears up. This is as big a moment for her as it is for Ivy.

They lower their voices as they hold tight to one another. I take a moment to gaze around the shop at the display cases and the pretty jewelry that sits inside.

A tap on my shoulder turns my attention back to Ivy and Linny.

"You have to be Athena." Ivy looks me over. "You're just as beautiful as Linny said you'd be."

I offer the daises to her. "These are for you."

Her green eyes drop to the flowers in my hand. "They're beautiful. Daisies are my favorite."

I smile at Linny. She wiggles her brows and tosses me two thumbs up.

Ivy takes a step closer to me. Her gaze drops from my face to my neck.

"Athena's arrangements are so unique, Ivy." Linny starts her pitch. "I know that you pick up flowers now and again to bring into work, but Athena could take care of that for you twice a week."

Ivy nods, but her eyes are locked on my neck.

"The cost is very reasonable," Linny goes on even though we decided on the subway ride here that I'd handle the discussion about Wild Lilac. "Athena has a gallery online that you can look through if you're interested."

Ivy's gaze finally travels back up to my face. Her brows knit together.

Linny pushed too hard. Ivy probably thinks the only reason I tagged along this morning was to try and land her as a client. That was part of it, but I wanted to meet her.

She's accomplished what I want to. She's taken her passion and built a million-dollar business out of it.

I look down when I feel Ivy's hand brush against mine.

"That locket is breathtaking. The etched rose on the front is beautiful." Her voice comes out quiet. "Where did you get that?"

I close my eyes briefly. I can't tell her that my mom stole it from my father or that the rose gave me inspiration to pursue a career in floral design.

"It was a gift from Athena's mom," Linny says. "She gave it to her a long time ago."

Ivy turns to look at Linny. "How long ago?"

I answer because I don't want Linny to have to lie for me. "My mom got the locket twenty-four years ago."

That sets Ivy back a step. Her hand darts to her chest. "Do you know where she got it?"

Linny clears her throat. Whatever she's about to say won't be based in truth. I've held onto this gold chain and locket for dear life for years. I've avoided every question about where it came from or who is inside.

I've never owned its truth because I've tried to bury mine.

I can't anymore. I won't anymore.

"She got it from my father." I swallow hard. "They had just met. It was a one-night thing."

Ivy reaches forward to take my hand. "That locket was stolen from Finola Lera's gallery twenty-four years ago. She handmade it for her mother."

My free hand instinctively reaches up to grab the locket. I close my fist around it. "Who?"

"Finola Lera," Ivy repeats. "She's an incredible jewelry designer. My hero."

Is my father related to Finola Lera? Is that where my creativity comes from?

"She made two identical lockets for her parents." She points at my closed fist. "A gold one for her mother and a silver one for her father. His hung on a pocket chain."

"Did they have a son?" I blurt out the question without thinking.

Her head shakes slowly. "No children."

I try to piece together everything she's saying. She can't be right. The people inside are my grandparents. I've never vocalized that to anyone, but my heart has always believed it.

"They caught the man who stole the pieces when he tried to pawn the silver locket." Ivy looks to Linny. "Her parents' pictures were in both."

Linny's voice comes out in barely more than a whisper. "What do her parents look like?"

Linny has looked at the pictures in the locket at least a dozen times since we met. She's always hatching a plan to find them. For a time, she wanted to post their images on Facebook to ask for clues. I told her no. I wasn't ready.

Tears well in my eyes as I loosen my hand and open the locket.

Ivy leans forward. Her gaze narrows as she studies the images. When her hand leaps to her mouth, I know before she even says a word.

"I can't believe it." She squeezes my hand. "This is it. Athena, you have Finola Lera's locket."

# Chapter 45

### *Athena*

My father died in prison seven years ago.

He was locked up four different times. His last sentence was for attempted murder. Retaliation killed him. He was stabbed in the shower at a prison in Pennsylvania.

No one mourned his loss. He was buried in an unmarked grave.

Yesterday, after I found out about Finola Lera, I went to her gallery in midtown Manhattan.

I gave her the locket along with my heartfelt apologies.

She wanted to give me something in return, but I only asked for one thing. I needed the name of the man who had been convicted of the theft of the matching silver locket.

Antero Willman.

I sent that to Jeremy, and within three hours, he was at Wild Lilac with two mug shots on his phone.

I look like my dad.

My nose is the same as the one in the middle of his handsome face. My eyes shine the same color of blue.

That's where our similarities end.

He took from other people to feed his drug habit, and the night he met my mom, she took from him to supply her own.

I was born nine months later.

By the grace of God, she held onto that locket and gave it to me.

It's back where it belongs now, around the neck of Finola's mom.

I look up at the mirror in my bathroom. My fingers skim over the skin at the base of my neck.

It's bare now. I look different.

My phone chimes. I glance toward it. It's been sounding off all morning.

I know who it is.

Liam is looking for me.

He's been trying to reach me since yesterday.

I couldn't respond.

I needed time to accept who I am now. I'm not the girl with the lingering hope that there's a man out there who feels something is missing from his life, a man who wanted a daughter as much as she wanted a father.

I don't have a father. I'll never have a father, but I have a family who would do anything for me.

I run a successful business, and I'm in love.

I skim my hand over my hair and manage a small smile. Pointing a finger at my reflection, I whisper the only words that matter. "You're not them, Athena. You're you. Go live a life you can be proud of."

\*\*\*

"Why don't you take the day off on your birthday?" Leanna nudges my shoulder. "I'll handle things here that day."

I keep my eyes trained on the bouquet in front of me. It's for an anniversary and the man who ordered it was very specific about how he wants it to look. He attached an image of his wife's wedding bouquet to his online order. I take recreations very seriously. "You don't have to do that, Leanna. Besides, you don't work on weekends."

"I want to." She moves to stand next to me. "It's a Sunday, Athena. I'll call the girls in to help. We close by six on Sundays, so it's not a big deal."

The girls are our weekend assistants. Leanna was the one who hired them, so I have no doubt that she'll be able to convince them both to show up that day.

"You deserve it." She sighs. "Consider it my birthday gift to you."

"Your birthday?" A man's gruff voice interrupts. "When is that?"

I look up just as Leanna does.

"It's him," she whispers. "Look, Athena, it's him."

*It is him.*

"Liam," I say his name softly. "Hi."

"Hi, yourself." He takes a step closer to the table.

Brushing my hands over the front of my jeans, I glance at Leanna before I gaze back at him. "What are you doing here?"

"I missed you." He shoves a hand through his hair. "I wanted to see your beautiful face."

"Swoon," Leanna whispers in my ear. "It's break time, boss. Don't hurry back."

It's not break time. It's the middle of the afternoon, and she's set to leave in less than an hour. I have two more orders to fill before Al shows up to pick her and the day's deliveries up.

"I have a lot to do," I say, glancing up at Liam. "Can we meet up later?"

"You have nothing to do." Leanna pushes my shoulder. "I'll take care of all of this. You take care of yourself."

"Give me ten minutes, Athena." Liam flashes me a smile.

How can I deny him anything when he's looking at me like that?

"Ten minutes," I repeat back.

"Make it thirty." Leanna laughs before she lowers her voice and turns to face me. "Take him home with you, Athena. An afternoon quickie might be just what you need."

I glance at Liam to find his eyebrows perked. When I look back at Leanna, she's shrugging a shoulder.

"He heard every word of that," I point out.

"Good." She winks. "Have fun, and don't hurry back."

# Chapter 46

### *Liam*

Reading people is something I've always been good at. It started when I was a kid, and my mom would sit in silence in her chair in the corner of her bedroom.

She'd pretend to be reading, but she bookmarked the same page for months.

I'd watch from my spot in the center of her bed where I'd sit and play with my toys.

She never turned a page. She rarely looked at the book.

She'd stare out the window for hours.

I didn't know why until a few years ago. She's never confided in me. Winola told me that sometimes people think they've reached a point of no return where their secrets have to stay buried.

That's bullshit.

It's never too late to admit your sins and cleanse your soul.

If the person listening to your confession loves you, they'll steer you into the light of forgiveness.

I want to do that with my mom but she chose to hide behind the truth she created in her mind.

Athena is hiding something too.

She hasn't said a word since we left Wild Lilac.

I strolled next to her, holding her hand while she looked off in the distance.

If there's another man in the picture, I'll fight for her. Dammit, I will beg her on bended knee to give me a chance to love her.

I'm ready for that. I need that.

I'll do whatever the fuck I can to sort my own life so I can start one with her that will last until we're both old and gray.

She opens the door of her apartment and steps inside. I follow, locking the door behind me.

I'm not going to make a move.

I hoped that I'd get to feel her body against mine at some point today, but she needs something else from me.

Understanding, or support. Hell, maybe she just needs silence.

Her fingertips dance over the front of her neck.

It's bare.

"Where's your locket?" I blurt out.

Her bottom lip quivers. "It was never my locket."

That makes no sense. "What do you mean it was never your locket?"

Her gaze trails over my face. "We don't have to talk about this."

"I want to talk about it."

She takes a full step back. "We've never talked about our lives or anything serious, Liam."

She's right. We've kept this on the surface, but I want it to be more. I fucking need it to be more because I want to tell her my truth.

I stalk toward her. "I care about you. I want to be here for you."

Her fingers trail over her neck. "Are you sure? This is so messed up."

It can't be more messed up than the hell I've been living in.

"Tell me." I cup her cheeks in my hands. "Tell me, lilac."

Her eyes fill with tears. "My mom stole that locket from my dad on the night I was conceived. She's in prison now but not for that. For other things; bad things."

Her mom isn't a saint. I know that from what Audrey shared.

Biting her bottom lip, she sighs. "The pictures in the locket were of a man and a woman. I thought they were my grandparents."

Makes sense to me.

"Where's the locket now?" I gaze around the room.

"It was stolen from a gallery twenty-four years ago." She closes her eyes. "It belongs to a jewelry designer. Her parents' pictures are in it."

*Fuck.*

"I took it back to her." She exhales. "She gave me the name of the thief; my dad. He died a few years ago."

I gather her in my arms, pressing her cheek to my chest. "I'm sorry, Athena. Jesus, I am so fucking sorry."

"I know now," she whispers. "At least, I know where I come from."

This is the point where I tell her my story.

I step back so I can look down at her. "Athena."

Her eyes find mine. "I'm going to be okay."

I nod. "You're strong. Listen, I want to tell…"

"My birthday is next Sunday," she blurts out. "We're having dinner at Nova. My family is having dinner there at seven. I'd like you to come."

I swear to God, my heart stalls inside my chest.

I know this has to be big for her. It's big for me. I don't hesitate because this is the first step on a path I want to take. I want a future with her. I need a future with her.

My past can wait.

"I'll be there, lilac."

She leans up to sweep her lips over mine in a soft kiss. "Thank you, Liam."

*Thank you, Athena, for giving me a reason to hope.*

I hold onto those words as we fall onto her bed, and her hands drop to my belt.

# Chapter 47

*Athena*

I rush back into Wild Lilac after spending an hour in bed with Liam.

He ate me to an orgasm before I sucked him off.

He didn't have a condom, and the ones I still have in my nightstand drawer wouldn't fit.

He tried, and we laughed at the fact that they were too small.

It didn't matter.

It was still magical and perfect in every possible way.

I walked back to the store feeling as though a weight had been lifted off my shoulders. Liam knows that my parents have made horrible mistakes, but he didn't judge me because of them.

I still saw adoration in his gaze. I still felt tenderness in his touch.

He agreed to meet my family next week.

Maybe my twenty-fourth birthday will be the start of the best year of my life.

"You're back," Leanna singsongs from behind the table. "Your cheeks are flushed. Your hair is messed up. It looks like you had a good time with that gorgeous man of yours."

I fumble with something to say. "We...I..."

"You don't owe me an explanation." She sighs. "I think you should duck out of here more often to meet him."

I think so too.

"Al is on his way over." She points at the coolers. "I got everything done, so we are ready to hit the road for deliveries."

"What would I do without you?"

She tilts her head. "You'll never find that out. I plan on sticking it out until the day I die."

I can only hope that's the truth.

"I'll take you up on that offer for my birthday." I smile. "I want to take the day to get ready for a very special dinner my family has planned."

Narrowing her gaze, she studies my face. "I hope Liam will be there."

Hearing his name come from her lips so effortlessly keeps the smile on my face. "He will be."

"Mark my words, Athena." She crosses her arms over her chest. "By this time next year, you'll have a diamond ring on that finger."

I glance down at my left hand. "One day at a time, Leanna."

"An assistant can dream, right?" She flashes her wedding ring. "When he does pop the question, promise me that you'll let me help with the flowers for your big day."

"I promise," I sound back even though I don't want to tempt fate.

Liam and I are a long way from exchanging vows. We haven't even said *I love you* to each other yet, but I feel it inside. After today, I think he might too.

\*\*\*

"You like this guy a lot, don't you?" Jeremy leans his hip against the kitchen counter in my apartment.

It's late.

I've worked non-stop for the past few days because I booked a last minute wedding.

The original florist bailed, so the bride came to me in tears three days ago.

I was still wallowing in the lingering grief of finding out the truth about my father when she walked into the shop.

I sat her down, went over what she envisioned for her wedding, and I set out to make it happen.

It took calls to three different suppliers on the east coast, but I pulled it off.

Leanna worked late the last few nights, and we had to reschedule the drop-in flower arranging class, but we got the job done.

"Liam is a good man." I take a sip of water. "You'll like him, Jer."

He nudges the bag of food he brought with him toward me. "You should eat something, Athena."

"Leanna ordered pizza." I glance into the brown paper bag. "I'll make a sandwich before I go to bed."

"Can you see yourself marrying him?"

I choke on the last swallow of water in the bottle. I cough once and then again as I wag a finger at my brother. "Don't go there."

I don't mention the fact that Leanna is still driving the marriage train at high speed. She's mentioned it at least once a day since Liam came into Wild Lilac. I haven't seen him since. I pointed out that fact to her, but she laughed and told me that absence makes the heart grow fonder.

"We are dating," I say on a wheeze. "Promise me that you won't bring up marriage at my birthday dinner."

His hand dives into the bag. "I promise. I'm putting this food away, and then I'm taking off. Eat and then sleep, Athena."

I need to fit a call to Liam in there too, but I don't tell my brother that.

"I'll see you on Sunday," I say with a smile. "You'll be on your best behavior, right?"

"I'll be a charming son-of-a-bitch." He flashes an over-the-top smile. "Tell your boyfriend that if he doesn't show up, I'll hunt him down."

"He'll be there," I reassure him with a kiss on the cheek. "He promised me that he would be there."

# Chapter 48

### *Liam*

"Fuck." The word falls from my lips as my call to Athena drifts to her voicemail.

We haven't connected in days.

Her rush to get the flowers done for a last-minute wedding and my overbooked schedule haven't given us a chance to connect other than via text message.

One of my colleagues came down with the flu, so I took on her clients as well as my own.

I've been in the office from sunrise to sunset for the last five days.

I'm tempted to reschedule the basketball court session I'm on my way to, but Gareth Quillan is ready and willing to meet up, so I need to show up for him and his son.

I adjust the waistband of the black shorts I'm wearing. I tugged a black hoodie on with it because the wind has been whipping its way through Manhattan today.

Tying my hair back isn't something I do much of anymore, but if I'm going to stand a chance on the court today, I need a clear path of vision.

I try Athena one last time before I toss my phone in the backpack slung over my shoulder.

There are a thousand things I want to say to her starting with I love you.

It's time.

I feel it inside, so why not share it with her?

I'm hoping that those three words and the gift I'm getting for her birthday will be enough to cement a place in her life for the long haul.

If I thought I stood a chance of her saying yes, I'd ask her to marry me.

I'm gone for this woman. My heart belongs to her.

I need to step up and take care of a few things so it'll be hers forever.

I round the corner toward the basketball court when a wave of dizziness hits me.

I didn't stop for lunch today, and dinner is at least an hour away.

I level my steps with a hand on the back of a bench. A few deep breaths help, but I drop to the seat and close my eyes.

I'm running on empty. I know it. I've stretched myself too thin the last few months.

"Hey, Wolf!"

I recognize Rhys's voice, so I raise a hand when I look to the left.

He's standing at the entrance to the court.

"I'm on my way," I call back, taking an extra two seconds to catch my breath.

"My old man will go easy on you." He yells. "He'll spot you ten points."

I may need it.

I push to my feet and set off toward Rhys and his bright blue hair.

I give the kid credit for honoring his mom in the best way he knows how.

When I reach him, he goes in for a side hug, so I accommodate with a slap in the middle of his back.

"Wolf," he says my name in a shaky tone. "I want you to meet my dad."

I spin around to face the man that owned the heart of Deidre Quillan. The man she met in grade school, fought with through middle school and fell in love with in high school.

Steely blue eyes and short cut dirty blond hair greet me. A hand is shoved at me as he studies my face. "I'm Gareth."

"Liam Wolf." I take his hand in mine for a shake. "I already feel like I know you."

When I try and tug my hand away, he holds on for a beat too long. "I feel the same way, Liam. I feel the same way about you."

***

Two hours later, I stand in front of Wild Lilac and stare in the windows.

Fate brought me here weeks ago. That's the only way I can explain any of this.

Athena's past is as twisted as mine.

I drop a hand to the handle and tug on it.

I don't give a shit that I'm covered in sweat and that my heart took a bigger beating on that court than my body did.

Watching Rhys with Gareth was humbling.

Deidre lost more than I realized when she took her last breath in that hospital bed.

She missed the chance to see her son fall in love. She lost every opportunity she could have had to sit down and talk with him one-to-one about life and choice and honor.

I step inside Athena's shop and gaze around.

I don't recognize anyone but Leanna, the woman who was here last week when I stopped in to see lilac.

"Liam." She drops the flowers in her hand and approaches me. "Can I help you?"

"Where's Athena?"

"Setting up for a wedding." She gives me a once over. "I'm heading over there in twenty minutes to help."

I want to know where it is so I can go there and wrap myself around her. I want her to chase away all the pain that's been living inside of me for years. I want a fresh start with her and I want to give her the same.

"I'll tell her that you stopped by," she offers. "I can ask her to call you when we're done."

I give her a curt nod. "Please."

Her hand moves to touch me, but she pulls back. "Can I help you with anything?"

Compassion swims in her tone. I know I must look like hell. I feel like it.

"Just let Athena know that I'd like to speak with her."

"Sure thing." She smiles. "I'll let her know."

I exit the shop and head across the street. It's time to face my future and leave my past behind. Tonight I'm taking the first step.

# Chapter 49

*Athena*

"You're sure he said that he wanted me to call him?" I glance down at my phone even though the question is directed at Leanna.

"Yes," she says solemnly. "I can tell you word-for-word what he said that night, Athena."

*That night.*

It was days ago.

I was busy prepping the flowers for the last minute wedding order. Liam dropped by Wild Lilac.

Leanna said he was dripping in sweat and seemed on edge. He asked her to relay a message to me that he wanted to talk. She forgot to tell me until the next morning because we were both so focused on setting up the wedding flowers.

Twelve calls and close to twenty text messages later, and I still haven't heard a word from him.

I even stopped by the Dehaven Center. A temp was sitting in Audrey's chair since she had scheduled a few days off for a girls' trip with her sister before the wedding.

The only thing the man sitting behind the reception desk would tell me was that Liam was unavailable.

"There's an explanation for this." Leanna sets a lily in the middle of an arrangement before she tugs it back out. "He hasn't ghosted you, Athena."

She just gave a voice to my biggest fear.

Today is my birthday.

I'm having dinner with my family in six hours at Nova, and I haven't seen or heard from the man I love.

"You're supposed to be at home getting ready for tonight." She taps me on my hip. "Go and do that. I'll cover things here."

I'm here because I can't spend another second at home alone.

I've been to Liam's apartment building twice, but I couldn't get inside. I've done everything in my power to reach out to him.

"He knows about my mom," I confess quietly. "I told him about my mom and my dad."

"Your dad?" Leanna sets a hand on my shoulder. "You've never mentioned your dad before."

I haven't mentioned my mom to her either, but most of Manhattan knows the name Simone Millett.

"He wasn't a great man." I look up at the ceiling. "I told Liam about that. Do you think…"

"No," she answers before I can finish my question. "He doesn't strike me as the type of man to dump a woman because her parents are screwed up."

She doesn't know him.

I do, and I have no idea if he's that type of man.

I wanted to believe he wasn't, but reality is forcing me to accept that he might be.

"What am I supposed to do about tonight?" I ask, scrubbing a hand over the back of my neck. "My family thinks they are meeting him."

Her hands find mine. "Athena, they love you. They love you so much. They'll understand. Be honest with them, and they'll understand."

It's advice I need to follow, but first I have to do the impossible.

I need to be honest with myself that Liam Wolf may not be the man I thought he was.

\*\*\*

Hope is a fool's currency.

I'm holding onto it as though my life depends on it.

I'm in the bathroom at Nova. My family is seated at the table waiting for Liam to arrive.

I held my breath as I made my way to the restaurant. Holding out hope isn't easy when your phone doesn't ring.

Glancing around the vacant washroom, I scroll through my contact list until I find Liam's number.

I hit dial.

If my past brought me to this point, so be it, but this man needs to know that he's a coward. He has to know that judging me based on who my parents are is wrong.

I smooth my hand over the skirt of my black dress as his phone rings and rings.

Finally, on the sixth ring, the familiar sound of his voicemail message kicks in.

I listen to the same words I've heard countless times the past few days.

Once I hear, "*I'll get back to you*," and the tone sounds, I start talking.

"This is the last time you'll ever hear from me." I take a breath. "The very last time."

My gaze drops to the floor as I pause. "I thought you were a decent person. I get that you can't accept me because of who my parents are, but you could have at the very least said goodbye to me."

The sound of the bathroom door opening behind me drops my tone. "It's my birthday. I'm at Nova with my family, and they're waiting to meet you. Goodbye, Liam. Don't call me back."

I end the call with tears threatening to fall.

"Seriously?" A vaguely familiar voice asks from behind me. "You're that flower girl. Don't tell me that you were just talking to Liam Wolf?"

It can't be. Please don't let it be Wren.

"It's Athena, right?" Her voice gets louder as she nears me. "Audrey told me that you two hung out with her and Jay. What's going on with you and Wolf?"

I spin around to answer her honestly. "Nothing."

Her finger circles the air in front of my face. "You're about to cry. Is it because of him?"

I don't answer her. I can't.

"I heard you say that it's your birthday." Her gaze drops to the phone in my hand. "You're waiting for him, aren't you? He didn't show."

I refuse to give her the satisfaction of knowing that Liam dumped me.

"Listen to me." She steps closer. "This is what he does. He disappears when you need him. I wanted him to meet my folks when they were in town and he had a session and then another. It was one lame excuse after another until he went radio silent."

I want to ask her if that's why she refused the flowers he sent her, but I see the answer in her eyes. I also see anger there and concern.

"Don't let him do this to you." She shakes her head. "You're better than this."

I watch as she adjusts the neckline of the red dress she's wearing.

"I'm here tonight with a man who appreciates me." She smiles. "He's never stood me up. Don't you deserve the same?"

Damn right, I do.

I march past her and exit the washroom. I'm here to celebrate my birthday with my family and I intend to do just that.

# Chapter 50

*Athena*

"Tell me what it's like being twenty-four." Leanna drops a cupcake in front of me. "It's been a decade for me, so I can't remember."

I manage a small smile. "It's only been a day for me, and I'd say so far, not so good."

I'm not saying that because I still haven't heard a word from Liam. I didn't expect to.

I made it very clear in that last voicemail message I left him that I was done.

After I had dinner with my family, I explained to them that Liam and I weren't going to work out.

I didn't get into the details of being ghosted.

Jeremy loves me to death, and as much as I appreciate his need to defend me, I didn't want to hear about how Liam had wronged me.

The details about what happened between us don't matter. The end result does.

We had fun, and then it was over.

I opened up and shared a part of myself that he couldn't handle. I may have second-guessed my decision to do that the past few days, but I don't anymore.

I'm the daughter of two people who made terrible choices.

That doesn't define me. If anything, it has helped me see that I can do better.

"I didn't sleep much last night," I clarify my previous comment so Leanna doesn't start asking about Liam.

"All the sugar in this will help." She points at the cupcake. "I ate mine on the way to work."

I manage a small laugh. "It was your breakfast?"

"I had breakfast early." She rubs her stomach. "The cupcake was for the little one in here."

I drop my gaze to the front of her jeans. "You're pregnant?"

"It's so early." She lets out a sigh. "I did the test at home this morning, so I'm still in the danger zone, but fingers crossed that next summer, I'll be a mom again."

I round the table to hug her. "I'm happy for you and Al."

She breaks the embrace to look into my eyes. "You'll get this too one day, Athena. The right guy will stroll through that door and sweep you off your feet when you least expect it."

That already happened.

I was swept away. I fell in love, and then he disappeared.

\*\*\*

Hours later, I finally lock the door for the day.

It was busier than usual. Leanna stayed an extra hour to help me fulfill all the orders that arrived before delivery cut-off. I helped Al load them into the back of his SUV before I gave them both a hug and sent them on their way.

I suck in a deep breath knowing that I am less than thirty minutes away from a bubble bath.

I set off to shut off the lights when a light knock at the door stops me in place.

Fear buckles through me.

I want it to be Liam as much as I don't want it to be.

I don't even know what I'd say to him at this point.

Another knock turns me around because I can't ignore it.

The man standing on the other side of the door is tall with black hair.

I inch closer and point at my watch, signaling to him that the store is closed for the day.

He points at the handle and tugs at it.

I shake my head and mouth the words, *"we're closed."*

His hand disappears inside his suit jacket, and for the briefest of moments, I wonder if he's about to rob me.

Something gold flashes in the air, but it's not a weapon.

It's a police badge.

I take a step closer to the door.

He raps his fist against it harder. "Open the door."

I do as he asks. I rush the rest of the distance to the door and flip the lock open.

He's yanked the door open before I have a chance to give it a push.

"Are you Athena?" He brushes past me. "You're Athena, aren't you?"

I nod. "Yes."

"Thank Christ." He pushes a hand through his hair. "We've been trying to find you for days."

I study his face and his bright blue eyes. Why does he look familiar to me?

"You've been trying to find me?"

"It's Liam." His voice cracks. "Something happened."

A sudden wave of nausea hits me with so much force that I stumble forward.

The man reaches both hands to steady me. "Are you alright?"

"Liam," I whisper his name. "Is he alright?"

"I need you to come with me." He jerks a thumb to a car parked on the street in front of the store. "Get what you need and come with me now."

I don't ask another question.

I race to grab my bag and my purse. With shaking hands, I lock the shop's door and slide into the front seat of the sedan next to the black-haired man.

Once the car starts and he's pulled out into the street, he glances at me. "I'm Sebastian Wolf. I'm Liam's brother."

The question I want to ask is buried beneath the lump in my throat.

Please let Liam be alive.

Please, God, let him be okay.

Give me a chance to tell him I love him.

# Chapter 51

*Athena*

I sprint through the hospital with Sebastian Wolf on my heel.

Once we pulled into a parking spot he told me where we were headed.

I was out of the car before he had his seat belt unbuckled. He called after me to get to the sixth floor.

There was a small crowd gathered at the bank of elevators in the lobby, so I took the stairs.

I'm racing forward without any clear direction.

All I know is that I need to get to the cardiac intensive care unit.

"Next right," Sebastian yells from behind me. "Then the next left after that."

I nod my head even though I have no idea if he's noticing.

"Right," he calls out as I head toward a dead end.

My boot slips on the tile floor as I turn sharply to the right.

I stop when I notice a group of people standing in what looks like a waiting area.

I recognize every face from the picture hung on Liam's wall.

"I found her," Sebastian calls from behind me. "That's her."

All eyes in the waiting room lock on me. I stare at them, willing someone to tell me where Liam is.

A short woman with brown curls approaches me with open arms. "Athena?"

I run to her because I need the comfort. I need the reassurance that the man I love will leave this hospital holding my hand.

"I'm Athena," I whisper to her.

"I'm so happy you're here," she says in a gentle voice. "I'm Wolf's mom."

A tear falls down my cheek. "You're his mom."

She steps back. Her hands tremble as she cradles my cheeks. "We've been looking for you for days."

*Days.*

How long has he been here? Why is he here?

The only thing Sebastian told me when we pulled into the parking lot was that his brother was brought in by ambulance a few days ago.

I search the faces behind her. "I want to see him."

A woman who can't be much older than me, approaches. "I'm Tilly Wolf."

*Tilly.*

We've met. I swear that I've met her but her name was...

Tilly Baker.

"My friend, Kate, owns the bridal shop next door to your store." She sighs. "She's the one who realized we've been looking for you. All we had to go on was the name Athena."

I step around Liam's mom to stand in front of Tilly. "Please tell me what's happening. Is he alright?"

Her hands find mine. She gives them both a squeeze. "He had surgery, Athena. Open heart surgery yesterday."

My chest feels like it's collapsing from the inside out. I struggle to find my next breath.

"Sit." She tugs on my hands. "Sit."

I lower myself into a chair. "Surgery? I don't understand."

"He went into cardiac arrest on the sidewalk a block from his apartment a few days ago." Tilly looks to Sebastian before she turns her attention back to me. "Luckily, a doctor was one of the first people on scene. He performed CPR until the EMTs arrived."

My hand jumps to my mouth as I let out a sob.

"Liam has a heart condition. It's called hypertrophic cardiomyopathy," Tilly goes on. "Part of his heart had become thickened."

"None of us knew." Sebastian crouches in front of me. "He found out a couple of years ago and kept it to himself."

"I was having coffee with him a few weeks ago when he felt faint." Tilly shakes her head. "I insisted he come in to be checked out. I left him here alone in the ER because I was feeling so nauseous. I had just found out I was pregnant the day before and the morning sickness was beating me up. I wish I had stayed. Maybe he would have confided in me."

Sebastian reaches for Tilly's hand. "You brought him in. You did your part."

Tilly nods. "When I checked in with him that night he said it was nothing. I didn't push. He's been dealing with this all alone for so long."

Tears fall down my cheeks.

"They had to stabilize him before they could perform the surgery." Sebastian smiles. "He's going to need some time to recover, but he'll get through this."

Relief pulls me forward on the chair. "Does he want to see me?"

A chorus of laughter echoes off the walls.

"Does he ever." Another man with black hair steps forward. "I'm Nick. Wolf's other brother."

"We figure he was out for a run the morning it happened." Sebastian sighs. "He didn't have his phone or ID on him. His wallet was in his apartment but the phone is gone. It looks like someone grabbed it when he collapsed. It took some time for us to connect with the doctors here. He came in as a John Doe."

I bury my face in my hands.

All those voicemails I left and the text messages.

None of those were reaching Liam.

"He's sleeping." Nick moves to stand next to me. "He'd like if it you were there when he wakes up."

"I'd like that too." I push to stand.

"We'll get you a gown and a mask." Sebastian motions to a woman wearing green scrubs. "He may look a little different than the last time you saw him, Athena."

I run a finger down the front of my sweater. "Is the scar from the surgery large?"

He nods. "It is, but that's not what I'm talking about."

I look around the room at the people listening to our conversation. "What are you talking about?"

"I'll let you see for yourself."

# Chapter 52

*Athena*

Tubes and machines are the first things I notice when a nurse takes Sebastian and me into Liam's room.

It's silent except for the loud beeps coming from the machines.

I take those sounds as a good sign.

Sebastian steps around me to approach the bed where Liam is. He's on his back. Tubes are coming from his chest, and an IV is attached to his arm.

His beautiful blue eyes are closed, but I see it.

I see what Sebastian meant when he said that Liam looks different.

His brother bends down. With a swift pull of the mask over his mouth down, he kisses Liam's forehead. "I found her, Wolf. I found Athena."

Liam's eyelids stay shut.

The machine beeps on as Sebastian turns to face me.

"He kept saying Athena," he says through the green mask. "He was in and out of consciousness before the surgery, but he only said two things. Your name and lilac."

My eyes fill with tears again.

I nod. "He calls me that."

"You're important to him."

My heart flutters with those words. "He's the most important person in my world."

"You love him?"

I don't hesitate when I answer. "With every piece of my heart."

A single tear rolls down his cheek. "We got another chance with him. I think he fought to stay alive because of you."

I step closer until I'm almost next to Sebastian.

I gaze down at Liam.

His beard is gone. His hair is much shorter. It's still long enough to fall onto his forehead, but the sides are trimmed close to his head. The back must be too.

"I called every hospital when I couldn't find him." Sebastian runs a gloved finger over his brother's cheek. "I described him, but he didn't match the bearded, long-haired guy I was looking for."

I stare at Liam.

"Once I called back and added the details about his height and the tattoos, I struck gold."

I nod.

"Did he look like this the last time you saw him?"

"No," I whisper. "He didn't."

"He's a handsome bastard, isn't he?" He huffs out a laugh.

Moving even closer, I slide a finger over Liam's smooth chin. "He's the most handsome man I've ever known."

\*\*\*

Time stalls when Liam's eyelids finally flutter open.

I move to stand next to him.

I've been here all night. Maybe it's been longer. This room doesn't have any windows, and my cell phone wasn't allowed, so Tilly promised she'd keep it safe in her purse.

I didn't need it.

I texted Jeremy to tell him what was happening before I came back in to settle into a chair for the night.

Liam's parents kept vigil in the waiting room, but they insisted that I take the chair in his room.

"*It's what my boy would want,*" his dad said.

"Liam," I whisper his name. "Please open your eyes."

One lid cracks open. His voice comes out in a growl. "Lilac?"

My breath catches in my chest at the sound of that. I'll never tire of hearing him call me that.

"I'm here." I lean closer. "I'm here, Liam."

His other eye opens a touch. "Pull that down."

I tug the mask down so he can see my entire face. I know I look like hell. I spent half the night in tears, both happy and sad. I spent the rest of the time trying to sleep, but I couldn't.

"You're beautiful," he whispers. "Look how beautiful."

"You are." I smooth a finger over his bare chin. "You had this face under all that hair."

He tries to laugh, but a cough escapes him. "You like this face?"

With the mask still down, I lean even closer. "I love this face."

His eyes find mine. "I love you."

I hold back the urge to kiss him because I don't know the risks and I won't jeopardize his recovery. Instead, I rest my lips against the soft skin of his cheek. "I love you, Liam."

Tears well in his eyes. "Say it again."

"I love you." I swallow hard. "I love you with my whole heart."

His lips tug up into a smile. "I love you with my whole heart. It's fixed now."

"I didn't know it was broken."

His gaze skims my face. "I have so much to tell you."

I kiss his forehead. "You will. I think you're supposed to rest now."

"You'll stay?" He bows his chin. "Will you stay until I wake up again?"

"I'm not going anywhere." I look to the door. "I won't go farther than the waiting room. I need to tell your mom and dad that you woke up."

"Tell them I love them, and it's okay."

"You love them, and you're okay," I say through tears.

"It's okay," he gently corrects me. "I know why they did it."

His eyes start to shut, so I don't press for more.

"I'll tell them," I whisper as I press my lips to his forehead. "I love you, Liam."

I love you, lilac. Happy Birthday."

# Chapter 53

*Liam*

One of those mail-in DNA kits altered my entire life.

Winola bought a bunch as a fun Christmas gift a few years ago. I swabbed the inside of my cheek and mailed it in.

When it came back, I read the results.

They didn't mirror the results that Nicholas had received back from the kit he'd sent it months before.

Not one damn thing matched.

I took that to my mother, but she laughed it off as a hoax.

"How can you trust something like that?" she asked. "They must mix up samples all the time."

It's plausible.

So I took it a step further.

When Sebastian crashed at my place for a weekend before he met Tilly, I tossed the toothbrush he used into a plastic baggie and dropped that off at a DNA lab in Manhattan along with another swab from inside my cheek.

A trained professional took that sample.

Our DNA didn't match.

Another visit to my mother followed along with another denial.

She pulled out a photo album filled with pictures of her pregnant with me.

She showed me the dated ultrasound image.

I accepted it all until I went to the doctor for a routine check-up and mentioned the shortness of breath I experienced when I worked out.

He ran tests, and then more tests.

The diagnosis was devastating.

I had a heart condition that was likely inherited.

The fact was that both my parents never had an issue. I asked.

It wasn't until I got my dad alone and shitfaced drunk that the truth spilled out of him.

The baby they were expecting died during childbirth.

My brothers and sister were waiting at home for their new baby brother to arrive, so when the teenager in the bed next to my mom mentioned that she was going to put her newborn son up for adoption, my parents stepped up.

It was all handled quietly with a lawyer that my dad had gone to high school with, and a check meant to help the teenage mother start over.

She and her boyfriend did just that after they kissed me goodbye and placed me in the Wolfs' arms.

They went to college, got married, and eventually had another son.

I look over at where Athena is asleep in the chair in my hospital room. She thought her parents fucked up. She has no idea.

"Lilac," I call out to her, knowing that it's cruel to wake her.

She stirs.

The hospital gown and mask are gone.

I've been cleared to touch the people I love. I'll be out of the ICU by tomorrow and home by the end of the week.

"Come here." I lean forward, but the tubes keep me in place. "I want you beside me."

She stretches. The T-shirt she's wearing rides up, revealing the barest hint of her smooth stomach underneath.

I can't fucking wait until I'm given the green light to make love to her.

I'll keep her in my bed for days when that happens.

"I can't believe I fell asleep." She pushes to stand. "When did you wake up?"

I have no clue. I don't know what time it is or what day. All I know is that she hasn't left my side.

She told me a day or two ago that her assistant has taken the reins at Wild Lilac. Leanna is her name, and she's brought in two retired florists to help fill orders. She wanted Athena to stay here, so she's doing what she can to make sure she has a business to go back to.

She smiles as she approaches my bed. "Your mom and dad went home a few hours ago."

I nod. They've been through the wringer since I landed in this place. I've never doubted their love for me. I'm their son in every way that matters.

"There was a man at the nurses' station earlier." She tugs on the bottom of her shirt. "Gareth is his name."

I didn't see that coming.

Her eyes zero in on mine. With a finger over her bottom lip, she smiles. "He has the same lips as you. The same color eyes too."

She's spent most of her life looking for a face like hers, so I'm not surprised she found mine in Gareth's.

"The nurse told him that only immediate family are allowed to see you." Her gaze darts to the door of the ICU. "He knew a lot about your condition because he has it too."

Her hand finds mine. "He's your biological father, isn't he?"

I nod, unable to form the words.

I knew it as soon as I locked eyes with him on the basketball court.

Gareth Quillan is my birth father. My birth mother, Deidre, died before I had a chance to thank her for gifting me with a life with the Wolf family.

"I told him I'd text him with an update." She sits on the bed next to me. "I hope that I didn't overstep."

I don't know if there's a relationship to be had between Gareth and me, but I want to find out. If he's open to it, I want Rhys to know that I'm his brother.

"You didn't," I assure her with a squeeze of my hand on her knee.

"We're more alike than I realized." She reaches for my hand. "Our parents aren't perfect."

"We'll do our best to do right by our kids."

Her head tilts. "Our kids?"

"I didn't think I could be a father." I pat my chest. "I didn't know how long I'd live before I met you."

Her gaze falls to the bandage on my chest.

"I knew I needed the surgery, but it was a risk I wasn't willing to take." I swallow hard. "The night before I collapsed, I had decided to go through with the surgery. I was set to book it, but fate stepped in and made it happen sooner rather than later."

She looks to the ceiling. "Thank you, fate."

"Thank you, fate, for bringing this woman into my life."

She leans forward to press her lips against mine. "I love you."

"I love you," I say to her. "Forever, lilac. Forever and a day."

# Chapter 54

## *Liam*

I'm bouncing off the walls in my apartment.

I've been home for a week. I've spent much of that time with my siblings and parents trying to work through our new reality.

I didn't see a need to wait to address the elephant in the room.

I may not have Wolf family blood running through my veins but I'm as much a son to my mom and dad as their other kids.

Nicholas and Sebastian took the news of my adoption better than I expected. Nikita's still processing and my mom went from vehement denial to begging me for forgiveness.

How do you forgive a person for giving you a life filled with love and support?

I thanked her over and over and promised her that I'd be her son until one of us takes our last breath.

My dad still can't recall his drunken confession.

He's sworn off everything but a beer on special occasions. That makes me wonder if there's more secrets buried deep inside of him.

If there are, they are his to live with.

Gareth and I have talked twice since I made it home. We'll meet up in a couple of weeks to have dinner with Rhys.

My younger brother knows about the sacrifice our parents made for me.

They weren't in a position to offer me anything but an uncertain future on the day I was born, so they put me into the loving arms of two people who were already raising three children.

I told Gareth I was grateful to him and Deidre.

He's thankful that I'm willing to give him a chance to be a friend now.

I glance down at the rectangular jewelry box in my hands. I was supposed to pick this up from Whispers of Grace, a jewelry store in SoHo, the morning of Athena's birthday but I was on my way to the operating room.

I got Sebastian to swing by there yesterday to grab it for me.

Tilly stopped by with a small chocolate cake earlier.

I'm all set for the small belated birthday celebration for the woman I love.

I turn from where I'm sitting on the couch when I hear her key in the lock.

She hasn't officially moved in yet, but she brought some of her clothing here and there are three flower bouquets brightening the space.

The door swings open with a kick of her boot against it.

I heave up to my feet to rush over to help her with the paper grocery bags in her arms and the bouquet of white roses she's balancing in one hand.

"Lilac." I plant a kiss on her forehead. "What the fuck is all this?"

"I'm cooking." She laughs. "One of the cardiac nurses pointed me to a website filled with heart healthy recipes."

We've been eating our way through the food my mom has prepared and dropped off since I was released from the hospital.

I peer inside the bags and mostly see green.

"There's some protein in here, right?" I scoop up both bags.

"Salmon." She kicks off one boot and then the other. "We'll have a kale salad with it and then a fruit tart for dessert."

"Chocolate cake for dessert."

"Yeah, no." She shakes her head as she takes off toward the kitchen. "There's too much sugar in cake."

I fall in step behind her. It's impossible not to stare at her ass in the faded jeans she's wearing or at her shoulder. It's peeking out from beneath the pink sweater that's sliding down her arm.

"It's your birthday cake."

She turns to face me. "What?"

I point at the coffee table and the cake. "It's over there."

"You went out?" Her voice trembles. "I thought we agreed that I'd go with you if you want to step out."

She's been hovering and I fucking love it. I know she's worried but I'm getting stronger by the day.

We're not that far out from the day I can take her to bed and ravish her.

I'm counting the goddamn hours until that happens.

Her eyes skim my face.

I took the step to rid myself of the beard and long hair the night I met Gareth. I've always known that the face under the beard didn't look like my parents or siblings.

I walked into the barbershop across the street from Wild Lilac and requested a shave and a haircut. By the time I stepped out of the chair, I felt like a new man.

The face I see in the mirror finally is familiar to me.

"Tilly brought the cake." I sigh. "Sebastian picked up your gift."

"There's a gift?" Her gaze drifts back to the table. "You didn't have to get me a gift, Liam. The surgery was the gift."

*It sure as hell was.*

I'm looking at years with her now. I can plan ahead, get married, have kids, live.

We're going to work toward that.

I tug on the bottom of the navy T-shirt I'm wearing. "How could I not get the woman I love a gift? It was supposed to be in your hand on your birthday."

"Do I have to wait until after dinner to have it?"

I huff out a laugh. "Fuck no. Come with me."

Her hand drops in mine. I press my lips to her palm before I tug her toward the sofa.

# Epilogue

## *7 months later*

## *Athena*

I gaze in the mirror at the gold locket hanging around my neck. The etched lilac on the front catches the light and shimmers.

I haven't taken the locket off since Liam put it around my neck the day he asked me to move in with him. It was almost two weeks after his surgery.

I ate a bite of chocolate cake before I opened the locket to find two pictures.

The one on the right is of me.

Liam must have taken it when I didn't realize it. I'm looking forward in it, but my eyes were fixed on something to the left of the camera.

The image on the left is of Liam.

Short hair, a rugged jawline, and those beautiful blue eyes of his.

I've stared at the images for hours on end.

This is the locket that was always meant to hang around my neck. It will always stay there.

"If you walk around naked, I'm going to have to take you back to bed."

I glance at the doorway to find my boyfriend completely naked too.

"We can't." I tilt my head. "We were supposed to be at the hospital an hour ago."

Before I can say another word, I'm up and over his shoulder. My protests about us being late are met with a slap on my ass.

"Liam," I cry out. "That hurt."

He tosses me onto my back on the bed before he crawls over me.

I zero in on the lust that's filling his eyes. "You want me."

"Jesus, lilac." His thick cock brushes against my thigh. "When the fuck do I not want you?"

I can't answer that. We make love at least once a day, sometimes more.

I'm often woken with the brush of his thick cock against my ass or his face between my legs.

We stopped using condoms months ago because I'm on birth control. The raw feeling of him inside of me is everything. I can't get enough of it.

I can't get enough of him. We both still work too much, but we set aside time every week for an entire day together. I've hired another florist full-time and another will help temporarily when Leanna starts her maternity leave.

"Fuck me now," I whisper.

"You're trying to kill me." He laughs. "My heart is strong, but when you talk like that, it stops. It fucking stops beating."

I dip a hand between my thighs. "I'm wet."

He glides down my body, trailing soft kisses over my skin. "I'll make you wetter."

My eyes drift closed as his tongue hones in on the tight bundle of nerves. The rest of the world can wait for us. This is exactly what we both need now.

\*\*\*

I tug on one of my boots.

"Liam," I yell from the bedroom. "Have you seen my other boot?"

"Under the bed," he calls back from the bathroom. "I think I might have kicked it under there when I was fucking you into tomorrow."

My pussy aches with those words.

It's still tender.

We're still late.

"Are you almost ready to go?" I tie the top of my black blouse in place.

I want to look nice today. First impressions are everything, so I want to look my best.

Brushing up behind me, he drops to his knees. "I'll find that damn boot."

I kiss the top of his head, relishing in the sight of him shirtless. "Thank you, babe."

I turn toward the closet to fetch my purse.

"Athena."

"What?" I call back over my shoulder.

"Turn around."

I spin in place and lose my balance almost immediately because of the sight in front of me.

"Oh my God," I whisper. "Liam."

He's on one knee. There is a small square box in his left palm. His right hand is firmly planted over the scar that runs the length of his chest.

"I had a speech." He huffs out a laugh. "But fuck it. I love you, lilac. Marry me. Please marry me."

I nod. "Yes, please."

The box pops open to reveal a small diamond nestled in a plain silver band. I've seen it before. We picked it out together at a market in Brooklyn one rainy Sunday afternoon weeks ago.

He promised he'd wait until my birthday to ask me, but I was hoping that he'd break that promise.

He slides back to his feet to slip the ring on my finger. With a kiss to the top of it, he smiles down at me. "We'll show everybody today."

"At the hospital?" I exhale. "Today is all about little Jacob Wolf."

Our nephew, Sebastian and Tilly's son, was born at six twenty-five this morning after seven hours of labor and dozens of phone calls between Liam and his siblings.

"Jacob won't mind." Liam tilts up my chin with his hand. "We'll kiss him, drop off some flowers for Tilly, and let the family know that there's a wedding in the very near future. I'll text Gareth and Rhys on the way to give them the good news."

"How soon do you want to get married?" I question with a perk of both brows. "I need at least a few months to get ready."

"You name the date, and I'll be there, lilac." He presses his lips to mine for a slow kiss. "I plan on being next to you for the rest of our lives."

I can't ask for more than that.

This man.

This love.

This life is everything I've ever wanted.

# THANK YOU

Thank you for purchasing and downloading my book. I can't even begin to put to words what it means to me. If you enjoyed it, please remember to write a review for it. Let me know your thoughts! I want to keep my readers happy.

For more information on new series and standalones, please visit my website, www.deborahbladon.com. There are book trailers and other goodies to check out.

If you want to chat with me personally, please LIKE my page on Facebook. I love connecting with all of my readers because without you, none of this would be possible.

www.facebook.com/authordeborahbladon

Thank you, for everything.

# ABOUT THE AUTHOR

Deborah Bladon has never read a romance hero she didn't like. Her love for romance novels began when she was old enough to board the bus, library card in hand to check out the newest Harlequin paperbacks. She's a Canadian by heart, and by passport, but you can often spot her in New York City sipping a latte and looking for inspiration for her next story. Manhattan is definitely her second home.

She cherishes her family and believes that each day is a gift for writing, for reading, and for loving.

Printed in Great Britain
by Amazon